# FORBIDDEN SPELL

First Edition Paperback
ISBN 978-1-7329865-0-3

Anadel Publishing
www.anadelbooks.com

Wholesale Distribution by Ingram

# CONTENTS

1: Anadel

2: New Arrival

3: Secret Books

4: Glowing Bottle

5: Forbidden Spell

6: Perfect Crime

7: Sparked Ambition

8: Missing Something

9: Preparations

10: Palace Key

11: Black Cat

12: The Karpat

13: The Knife

14: Trapped

15: Distraction

16: Flame and Fear

17: Big Mistake

18: The Truth

19: Confrontation

20: Broken Things

TALES OF ANADEL

# FORBIDDEN SPELL

JASON M SMITH

FOR OWEN

# 1: ANADEL

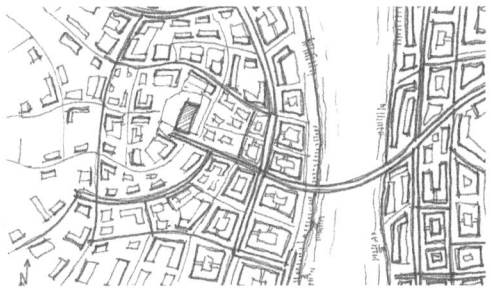

Milos Baran was sitting on his bed reading as he had been most of the day. As usual, everyone else in the palace was busy. At thirteen years old, he was the youngest person living in the palace by a decade. This meant that he was often on his own. Every once in a while he could get one or two of the staff to play koleso with him. But today everyone seemed to be especially busy and did not have time for throwing rings at the little posts he had set up in the courtyard.

He could try to ask his teacher Dimas. Dimas had no interest in playing koleso of course. He said that it was a game for commoners, only fit to be played by the people across the river. But Dimas was always willing to play a game of padat if he could spare the time. He felt that it was a noble game and that the son of a lord should be able to play it well. Milos thought padat was okay, but he preferred playing outside to pushing pieces around a padat board.

Dimas was nowhere to be found this morning anyway. Milos liked Dimas, but he hoped that he wouldn't see him for the rest of the day. That would mean he did not have to do his lessons. He preferred reading because he could read about whatever he wanted. Well, almost anything. His lessons were all about history, diplomacy, and all the other things Dimas and his father wanted him to learn.

His father, Lord Andrik Baran, was too busy to play games. He presided over the city of Anadel. Anadel was one of the greatest cities in the kingdom, mainly due to its influence over the Dan River. Much of the wealth of the kingdom traveled along the river through Anadel. Technically Andrik served the king. But the king lived far away in the capital, which was many weeks travel by boat up the Dan River.

Because Milos was the son of an important man, he was not usually allowed to leave the palace. He was certainly never allowed to go out alone, which from time to time he did under cover of night. When he managed to sneak away, he liked to explore the rolling hills and large estates to the west.

Milos had light brown hair and even lighter brown eyes. His eyes looked exactly like his father's. But his father's hair was dark with streaks of gray. Milos was told that his hair was the color of his mother's. He had to take their word for it since he had never seen it for himself. His mother had died when he was a baby. Milos was running his fingers through his sandy brown hair when there was a knock at the door.

Dimas opened the door and entered.

"It is time for your lesson," said Dimas curtly.

"What are we learning today?" Milos asked over the top of his book.

Dimas was holding several maps and books under his arm which he dropped onto Milos's desk.

"Today we will review the history of our city," he said. Milos rolled his eyes.

"I already know all that!" he said impatiently.

Dimas raised his eyebrows.

"Oh really? In that case, you wouldn't mind a little test," he replied.

Milos closed his book and sat up in his chair. He knew all about the city's history, and he was eager to prove it to Dimas. Dimas cleared his throat.

"Where does the city get its name?"

That was an easy one. Milos answered right away,

"The two ancient cities of Anad and Nel used to be on either side of the Dan River. When the cities grew, and the first bridges were built across the river, they became one city called Anadel."

Dimas turned and walked towards the window.

"Correct," he said, "Anad was built upon the hills on the west side of the river—"

"And Nel was built on the plains on the east side of the river," Milos interjected.

"Naturally. Now tell me, how long has the Baran family governed the city?"

"The King put my great-great-grandfather Miko Baran in charge after the King's army took the city in 1512," Milos replied.

Dimas raised his eyebrows again. He seemed impressed Milos knew the exact year.

"Very good," said Dimas, "now let's see."

Dimas brought his finger up to his lips as he thought. Milos was sure his teacher was trying to think of a harder question. Dimas reached towards the pile of books he had brought and picked one of them up. Milos recognized it. It was a book his father had written all about the city of Anadel before Milos was born.

Dimas held up the book so that Milos could see the cover.

"According to Lord Andrik Baran, what are the three greatest threats to the city of Anadel?"

Now this was a harder question. Milos had read his father's book about the city, but that was some time ago. What had it said about threats?

Then he gradually started to remember something.

"From outside the city! Attacks from our rivals!" said Milos.

Dimas gave a little nod.

"From Inside the city, the unrest of the people," Milos continued, "and...Um..."

What was the last one? The book had named a threat from outside the city, a threat from inside the city. What else could there be?

When Milos was unable to give the last answer, Dimas clicked his tongue to show his disappointment. He folded his arms across his chest.

"Outside the city, inside the city, and through the city." As Dimas spoke, Milos recalled what the book had said.

"That's right, through the city," Milos continued as though he had remembered all along. "The flow of energy through the city. Like the river!"

Dimas set the book back down on the stack and said, "That's right Milos, like the river. The water flows into the city, and water flows out of the city. If you have too much water flowing in, the city will flood. If there is too much going out, the river will dry up. There must be a balance."

Dimas turned back towards the window.

"But many forces flow through the city. Elemental forces like wind and water, economic forces like goods and money. Some forces are not always easy to perceive or understand. We must have respect for them. We must take care not to meddle with them, for they are all connected. That is why your father has banned the use of any magical arts in Anadel. The risk of disturbing the balance is too great."

Milos stood up and faced his teacher, "Is magic really so dangerous Dimas?" There was a mixture of curiosity and concern in his voice.

His teacher gave him a little smile and said, "Not to worry Milos. There's no need to worry about magic here in the palace."

Milos could tell he was avoiding the question. Dimas knew a lot about magic, and Milos was always eager to get information out of him on the subject.

Milos started to ask his teacher another question, but Dimas spoke first.

"Well since you already know all about the city, I will leave you to your books. I have a lot to do before tomorrow."

"What happens tomorrow?" asked Milos.

"Tomorrow the Lady Keren arrives to meet with your father," Dimas answered.

He turned to leave, but then stopped and turned back to Milos.

"Ah, that reminds me," he said smiling again "I understand the Lady Keren will be bringing her son with her. They tell me he is about your age."

Milos had not had any visitors his own age for a long time now.

"Really? What's his name?" Milos asked excitedly.

"No idea," Dimas replied with a little laugh.

"I will leave those with you," he said pointing to the books and maps on the table. "Maybe they will keep you busy until our guests arrive tomorrow."

Then Dimas stepped through the door and closed it behind him.

# 2: New Arrival

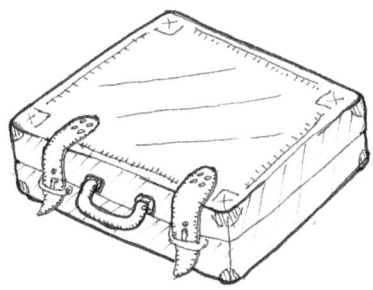

The next morning, Milos was woken by his teacher knocking on his door once again. This time Dimas did not open the door. He called to Milos from the hallway. "Milos! It is time to get up. You must be ready to greet our guests in the main hall in one hour!"

"I'm already up!" Milos called back to Dimas.

"Ha! I'm sure you are," Dimas said with a laugh. "Now get dressed and eat some breakfast while you still have time."

Milos jumped out of bed and opened the door to his closet. He pulled on a pair of soft white cotton pants and a long yellow silk shirt. He wrapped a brown belt around his waist and ran out of his room towards the kitchens. He was eager to meet the boy Dimas had told him about the day before, and he did not want to be late.

He arrived at the long wooden table that sat outside the kitchens. A plate of sausage and bread had been set out for him, along with a large cup of milk. He sat down and ate his food as quickly as he could. After scarfing down most of the food on his plate, he started to run out towards the main hall. Before he was three steps from the table, the kitchen door opened behind him.

The head of the house staff stepped out. Her name was Bina, though Milos liked to call her "Old Bina" because it annoyed her. She was old compared to him, but really she was no older than his father. Bina looked at Milos's plate and called to him before he could leave.

"By the stars! Surely you are not running off without finishing your milk?"

Milos stopped in his tracks and turned back towards Bina, rolling his eyes. Bina smiled and shook a stubby finger at Milos.

"Now boy, if you don't drink your milk, you'll never grow taller than Old Bina."

Milos couldn't help but smile at her words. He was almost as tall as Bina already. He ran back to the table and quickly drank the rest of the milk he had left behind.

Milos set the cup down hard and once again headed towards the main hall.

"And don't run so soon after eating!" Bina called after him.

But Milos turned down the vast hall and continued on at full speed. He did not stop until the long hallway opened up into a grand entrance hall at the front of the palace.

Only a few people were in the hall, standing at the foot of the large staircase that led up to the second floor. The twisted wrought iron handrails turned to become a railing along the second floor landing. Dimas was speaking quietly with two of his father's other advisers. Milos saw his father was not there yet, so he knew he must be early.

Dimas had come to the palace when Milos was a boy. He was a respected scholar who had studied in the capital. Andrik had brought him to Anadel to be Milos's tutor. Over the years he had also become one of Andrik's most trusted confidants. So his time was now split between Milos and his father. Dimas said he did not mind this on account of Milos being such a bright pupil. This made his duties as a tutor both enjoyable and easy. At least, that is what he had told Milos.

Milos slowed to a stop in the middle of the hall. When Dimas saw him, he turned towards him with a look of surprise on his face.

"You are here already? I worried you would be late," Dimas said.

He took a closer look at Milos as he stepped towards him.

"And what is that on your face, Milos?"

Milos rubbed his sleeve across his mouth and chin. There was still some milk there. Dimas shook his head.

"I hope your manners improve when our guests arrive. Please do not do anything to embarrass your father in front of Lady Keren."

Milos stood up straight at these words. He was about to tell Dimas that he would not do anything embarrassing. But before he could speak, a large pair of doors on the other side of the hall opened.

Through the doors stepped Lord Andrik. He was

speaking with someone as he walked through the doorway. It was a few moments before he noticed Milos standing in the middle of the hall.

"Ah, good" Andrik said when he saw him, "You are already here."

Andrik gave a little smile as he greeted Dimas with a nod. Apparently, they had shared the concern that Milos would be late.

Several other people followed Andrik out of the doors that lead to his personal study. They positioned themselves by the stairs next to Dimas. Once they were all gathered, Andrik placed his hand on Milos's shoulder and smiled. Then he turned to face the group

Andrik spoke loudly to them.

"Today we are welcoming guests from the city of Breen. They will be staying in the city for only a few days before continuing up the river towards the capital. Hopefully, their brief visit will give us the opportunity to improve our partnership. As we all know, our relationship with Breen has been strained for many years, but I see no reason for this to continue—"

As Andrik spoke, the front doors of the palace opened behind him, and a man ran forward. Andrik leaned towards the man as he whispered into his ear. Then he turned back to the group.

"They are almost here. Come let us greet our guests properly," he announced to the group.

Andrik shifted his hand to Milos's back and led him towards the front doors. The rest of the group followed behind Milos and Andrik.

The man who had delivered the message ran back towards the massive front doors and pulled them wide open. The hall filled with warm sunlight. They could hear many shuffling feet moving up the smooth stone steps outside. Finally, a small group of people rose up onto the wide landing outside the front door.

Leading the group was a tall, slender woman with long black hair. It fell about her shoulders which were draped in red and gold silk. Trailing behind her were several people, including a boy with the same dark hair and eyes as the woman leading the group. Lord Andrik took his hand off of Milos's back and stepped forward into the light streaming through the doorway.

14

He extended his hand warmly to the woman.

"Lady Keren, allow me to welcome you to Anadel," he said in a cheerful voice. Lady Keren extended her hand as well. Lord Andrik took her hand and kissed it.

"I hope you will enjoy your stay here," he added standing up straight again.

"I trust that I will, Lord Andrik," she replied. "I look forward to spending some time with you. We have many things to discuss."

Andrik smiled at Keren for a few moments before responding, "Please, allow me to introduce my son, Milos."

He motioned for Milos to step forward. Milos took two steps forward and stood up straight next to his father. He wanted to make a good impression. As Dimas had reminded him, it was his duty to represent his father's household.

"It is a pleasure to meet you," Milos said formally.

"And you as well, young master," Keren replied with a kind smile. "And let me introduce my son, this is Caleb."

Keren gestured to her side, and the dark haired

boy stepped forward. He gave Milos a little nod and then turned to Lord Andrik.

"It is an honor to meet you, sir," he said.

"The honor is mine," Lord Andrik replied.

Now that Milos could see Caleb up close, he saw that he was a bit taller than him and probably a few years older than him.

"Well, I'm sure you are tired from your journey," said Lord Andrik speaking again to Lady Keren, "Please, come into my study and have a cup of tea. I'm sure Milos would be happy to show Caleb around the palace while we talk."

"That sounds lovely," said Keren sweetly.

Andrik and Keren proceeded into the study, and a procession of people followed after them. Dimas was the last to enter the study. He gave Milos one last look and then closed the doors behind him.

# 3: Secret Books

Milos and Caleb were now standing alone in the entrance hall. Caleb was looking around the room with a bored expression on his face. Milos swung his arms back and forth trying to think of what to say. Milos had been nervous when he had to present himself to Lady Keren, but he was even more nervous now that he was alone with the tall dark-haired boy.

When Caleb was unable to find anything interesting in the hall, he turned his attention to Milos.

"So," Caleb said, "weren't you going to show me around?"

"Oh, yeah, of course," replied Milos. He was grateful that Caleb had broken the silence.

"Well," Milos continued, "this is the main hall...

obviously."

Caleb crossed his arms impatiently.

"Uh, right," Milos went on, "and through there are my father's rooms." He pointed towards the doors their parents had gone through. He felt he wasn't making a very good impression. Milos took a deep breath and stood up straight again.

"Okay, if you'll follow me," he said with as much confidence as he could muster. He led Caleb down the wide hall of the south wing. This hall ran down the center of the whole palace and was lined with paintings and sculptures. All the doors on the left side of the hallway were closed off since they lead into his father's private rooms.

On the right side of the hall, two pairs of glass doors led into large connecting rooms. These rooms were filled with instruments of all sorts. They were also filled with warm light from the large windows that looked out over the grounds behind the palace.

After walking through these rooms, Milos headed back down the wide hall towards the north wing. There were a dozen smaller rooms in the south wing, but he didn't think they were worth seeing. Caleb followed him looking around the different rooms. Milos pointed out the different spaces, but Caleb didn't appear to be paying much attention to him.

Milos made a loop through the north wing which included the ballroom with its massive crystal chandelier, the dining hall, and the kitchens where he had eaten breakfast. Bypassing a dozen more almost identical rooms, mostly used by the staff, they arrived in one of his favorite parts of the palace. The library.

The library was divided into two rooms. One room was large and extended all the way up to the roof. This room was wrapped entirely with bookshelves. In one corner of the room, a spiral staircase led up to a second level which was also covered with bookshelves. Every inch of the room was filled with books.

As Milos and Caleb passed through this room, Caleb seemed to show some real interest. Milos was excited he may finally have found something he had in common with the boy. He talked excitedly about how many different kinds of books they had in the library.

The boys then passed into the second part of the library. It was the long reading room that stretched along the front of the palace. Large windows filled the room with soft light. Plump armchairs provided many cozy places to read, including a pair of chairs by a fireplace at the left end of the room.

At the right end of the room was a pair of straight-backed chairs on either side of a padat table. Milos thought about what Dimas had said. According to him, playing padat showed you were noble and educated. This gave him an idea.

"Would you liked to play padat?" Milos asked

Caleb did not answer right away, but eventually said, Okay.

They each sat down at the padat table and began to play. Milos wanted to impress Caleb with his skill at the game. After several turns, he found Caleb was making some odd moves. Caleb did not spend much time thinking before making his moves the way he did.

They had only been playing for ten minutes when Milos captured Caleb's most important piece, the Raja. This meant Milos had won the game. Caleb crossed his arms and said, "Whatever, padat is a stupid game anyway."

Milos frowned. He had hoped to impress his guest, but Caleb didn't seem to care as much about padat as Dimas did.

For a moment, he thought of asking Caleb if he would like to play koleso instead. But again he remembered Dimas's words, that koleso was a game for common people. Caleb would probably laugh at him if he suggested it.

Finally, Milos said, "Well, we could go on with the tour. It's mostly bedrooms on the second floor". Then Milos had another idea.

"Or I could show you some interesting books in the library," he added quickly.

Milos thought of showing Caleb the book he had found that was full of colorful illustrations of birds from far off lands.

Caleb considered for a second, and then a sly look appeared on his face as he looked across the table at Milos. Milos started to get nervous again. Caleb leaned forward over the pieces on the padat table.

"Do you have any books about magic?" he asked in a low voice.

Milos was shocked at the question. "Oh, well, no. There aren't any books like that," he said.

"Ha! I didn't think so," said Caleb smiling, "I've heard your family is afraid of magic."

"That's not true!" Milos exclaimed.

"Oh yeah? Then why did you ban magic in the city?" Caleb replied.

Milos was growing irritated. He did not like the way Caleb was laughing at him. He hesitated for a moment and then took a deep breath.

"What I meant to say was, there aren't any books like that in the library," Milos said as he stood up, "Follow me."

Milos led Caleb back into the main hall. He stopped for a moment to make sure their parents were still occupied in his father's study. They could hear them talking behind the wooden doors. They made their way up the stairs and down the hall to Milos's room on the north side of the palace. Once he had quietly closed his bedroom door behind them, Milos locked the door. Then he walked across the room and got down on his hands and knees next to his bed.

When he saw what he was looking for, he reached out his hand and slid a wooden box out from under the bed. Milos stood up and carried the box over to his desk. He pushed aside the books and maps Dimas had left there the day before and set the box down in the center of the desk.

Then he hesitated. He turned back towards Caleb who was looking eagerly at the box. Milos gave him a severe look and said, "Listen, you have to promise you won't tell anyone what I'm about to show you."

"Yeah, of course not," said Caleb without taking his eyes off the box.

Milos was not sure he should trust Caleb, but he wanted to show Caleb that he was not afraid of anything. He hesitated for a few more moments, and then made up his mind. He turned back toward the box and opened the lid.

From inside the box, he pulled out two large books and set them on the desk. One of them was old with a circular pattern on the cover. Along the spine of the book was written, "Principa Notoria." The other book was even older, and the only markings on it were several strange runes inlaid with pale gold on the black leather cover. Caleb's eyes grew wide as he looked at this book. He pointed at it and asked, "Can I see that one?"

Milos handed it to him with a smile. He knew Caleb would be impressed with his secret books. Caleb slowly flipped through the pages. It was filled with more runes and elaborate diagrams. Milos had no idea what any of them meant, but he found the patterns and shapes fascinating.

After Caleb looked through the book for several minutes, he closed it and handed it back to Milos. He had that same sly look on his face again. "So," Caleb said as Milos took the book and set it carefully back on the table, "do you want to see some real magic?"

# 4: Glowing Bottle

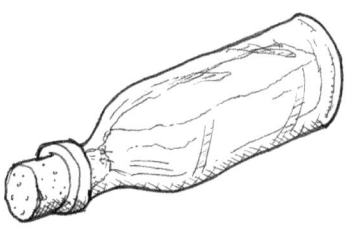

Milos stared at Caleb.

"What do you mean real magic?" Milos asked.

"I mean a real spell, like the ones in your book," Caleb replied eagerly.

Milos looked back at the book on the table. "You mean...you know how to use the symbols to do magic?" Milos asked. A strange mixture of fear and excitement was rising up inside his chest.

"Yeah!" said Caleb who was growing more excited. "I mean, I'm not sure about the stuff in that book," Caleb said as he pointed to the old leather book, "but I could show you one of the spells my mother taught me," Caleb added quickly.

Caleb reached out past Milos and picked up the other book. The one with the circular pattern on the front. "Here I'll show you," Caleb said. Milos took a step back.

"Show me what?" Milos asked nervously "are you going to do magic?"

"Don't be silly," Caleb said as he opened up the book and started searching through the pages.

Once Caleb found the page he was looking for, he handed the open book to Milos. Milos examined the pages. The page on the right was filled with a large circular pattern with a rune drawn on either side of it. The runes looked similar to the cover of the old leather book.

On the left page were several paragraphs written in a language Milos did not understand. Below the words were a series of smaller symbols. They looked like they might be pieces of the larger pattern on the opposite page. Caleb watched eagerly as Milos looked back and forth between the pages.

"Well, what do you say?" Caleb asked.

Milos was getting nervous now. Both Dimas and his father had told him that magic was dangerous. He may not have understood why, but one thing was for sure, this could get him in big trouble. Everyone knew you were not allowed to do magic in the city.

"I don't know, what if something goes wrong," Milos said trying to keep his tone casual.

Milos didn't want Caleb to think he was afraid. He was afraid, but not of magic. He was afraid of what his father would say if he caught them trying to do magic.

"Nothing's going to go wrong," Caleb said soothingly, "I've done it plenty of times, and it's always worked."

Caleb was examining the look on Milos's face.

"Come on," Caleb said encouragingly, "I know you want to see what it's like."

When Milos continued to stare silently at the book, Caleb pressed on, "It will be really small. No one will have any idea it even happened, trust me."

Milos had trusted Caleb enough to show him the books. It had been a pretty big risk. He had been so eager to impress Caleb that he had been careless. What if he told someone about the books? But now Caleb wanted to show Milos something in return. Something that could get them both in trouble.

At last, Milos looked up from the book, "Okay."

"Excellent!" exclaimed Caleb.

Milos sat the book back down on the table, still open to the page Caleb had shown him.

Milos took a deep breath trying to force down the anxiety that now reached up to his throat.

"So then...what do we do?" Milos asked, trying not to sound as nervous as he felt. Milos looked around the room, as though trying to decide the best spot to perform illegal magic.

"We can't do it in here," Caleb said as he watched Milos's eyes dart around the room.

"Besides, we don't even have anything to do the spell with," he added.

Milos stopped looking around the room and looked back at Caleb.

"Anything to do it with?" Milos asked confused. He tried to imagine what kind of things a person might use to do magic.

Caleb smirked at Milos, apparently enjoying the confused look on his face.

"Come on, you'll see what I mean," said Caleb.

They both stepped out of Milos's room and closed the door.

"We need to get to our carriage. Is there another way besides the front door?" asked Caleb.

"Yeah," Milos responded quietly, "we can go out the side door."

As he lead the way to the north stair, he was listening hard for the sound of footsteps. The way out through the north wing door would take them right past the kitchen. He was sure that if anyone saw them, they would know just by looking at them that they were up to something. Old Bina could always tell when Milos was hiding something. He hoped they would not run into her.

A lot of noise was coming from the kitchen doors as they passed by. The staff was busy preparing lunch for all the guests, and the boys slipped out the door unnoticed. Milos and Caleb edged around the wall towards the front of the palace. They arrived at the back of the carriage that had brought Lady Keren and Caleb to the palace.

Caleb carefully unlatched the door to a luggage compartment below the driver's seat. He pulled out a large leather case, set it on the ground, and unbuckled the straps that held it shut. Milos watched over Caleb's shoulder as he lifted the lid up until it laid back on its tarnished brass hinges.

Inside Milos could see a collection of books and papers. He watched in surprise as Caleb ignored the contents of the case, and instead put his fingers under the front lip of the lid. There was a muffled click. What had seemed to be the top of the case dropped down, revealing a thin secret compartment.

This compartment was lined with rows of small glass bottles held in place with leather straps. Caleb pulled out one of the bottles from the bottom row and pushed the panel of the secret compartment shut again. He closed the lid of the case and redid the straps. When the case was once again secured inside the storage compartment of the carriage, he turned back to Milos.

He held up the bottle to show Milos.

"Got it!" he said in an excited whisper. It was filled a thick blue liquid of some kind. Even though it was bright outside, Milos thought it seemed to be glowing. This time Caleb led the way as they headed back to the side door. Once they were both outside the door, he stopped.

"Okay, now all we need is a place to do this where

no one will notice," said Caleb. He thought for a second. "Do you have a basement or something?"

"Yeah, there's a cellar. It's full of wine and cheese and stuff," Milos said.

"That might work, let's check it out," Caleb replied.

"We can get down there from out here," Milos said. He led Caleb further down the side of the palace until they came to a pair of wooden doors that sat at a low angle up against the wall.

Milos grabbed a small handle and swung the metal crossbar to the side. He pulled the doors up and open and started down the steep stone steps. Caleb followed him and closed the doors behind them. Once the doors closed, it was suddenly dark.

Eventually, their eyes adjusted to the dim cellar. The only light came through narrow slits along the outside wall. Caleb looked around at the square room which was filled with dozens of dusty barrels and many shelves filled with stored food. On the other side of the room was a set of steep wooden steps that lead up into the kitchen.

"Yeah, this will work," Caleb said at last, "come

over here."

He walked over into the far corner of the room where it was darkest and sat down on the floor. Milos stepped quietly over to him and sat down beside him.

Caleb once again held up the small glass bottle. In the dark, Milos could see that the contents of the bottle were glowing with a blue light.

"What is it?" Milos asked in a hushed voice.

"Shhh, just watch," Caleb hissed back.

# 5: Forbidden Spell

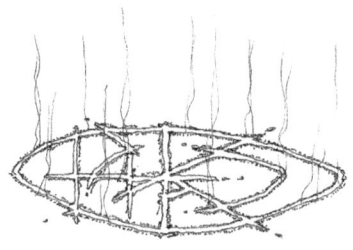

Caleb removed the small cork stopper from the mouth of the bottle. Then he placed his index finger over the top and turned it upside down. A moment later he flipped the bottle right side up again and pulled his finger away from the it.

Milos could see some of the glowing blue stuff on Caleb's finger. He placed his fingertip on the floor and then dragged it toward himself, leaving a bright blue line on the ground. Milos continued to watch intently as Caleb returned his finger to the opening of the bottle. He was not remotely afraid now. He was filled with anticipation.

Caleb repeated the same process several times, drawing a pattern of glowing blue lines on the stone floor. Then, with a sweeping motion, he drew a circle around the edges. Milos could see that the pattern on the floor was the same as the one Caleb had shown him in the book.

Caleb put more of the blue liquid on his fingertip and then looked over at Milos with that sly look on his face before returning his attention to the blue lines. He held his hand out over the circle and snapped his fingers.

A drop of blue liquid fell from between his thumb and index finger and landed in the middle of the circle. Slowly, the blue lines began to glow more and more brightly. A blue-white light filled the cellar. Milos watched in awe as wisps of smoke began to rise from the bright lines in front of him.

The circular pattern was now shining so brightly it appeared to be drawn on the floor with pure light. The light cast harsh shadows across the walls. The thick dust in the air of the musty cellar gleamed as though caught in a sunbeam. The smoke rising from the floor grew denser, and with a blue glow it wafted gently up to the vaulted stone ceiling.

Milos eyes grew wider as the dust and smoke began to revolve upwards in loose spirals. Soon a thick column of swirling smoke was extending up towards the ceiling, spinning faster and faster. Then without warning, there was a sudden rush of air as hot blue flames shot up from the circle in a tight spinning column.

Milos instinctively moved away from the fire. Still sitting on the ground, he pushed away from it with his hands and feet until his back was up against a heavy wooden barrel. He looked up with wide eyes at the rapidly twisting fire that now reached up to the ceiling. The flames fanned out across the arched ceiling in long tongues of flame that licked at the stones as if searching for a path upwards.

The fire and smoke persisted for a few more seconds, and then as fast as it had sprung up, it collapsed into the floor. For a moment, a smoky ghost of the pillar hung in the air above the circle. Milos briefly saw the shimmering lines on the ground through the smoke before they completely faded away. Then everything was dark again.

Milos's eyes had still not readjusted to the darkness when he heard Caleb's voice break the sudden silence in the cellar.

"Did you see that!" he said in an excited whisper. "I told you I could do it!"

When Milos did not say anything, Caleb stood

up.

"Well?" Caleb asked, "what did you think?"

"It..." began Milos breathlessly.

He was trying to think of the right words to describe it.

"It was...amazing," Milos said when he couldn't think of anything better to say.

"Yeah it was!" replied Caleb with a laugh. Milos continued to sit on the floor for a few more moments, then suddenly jumped to his feet. He had heard a noise from behind the door to the kitchen above. The sound brought him back to his senses. As though he had come out of a trance, reality seemed to rush back into the cellar.

"We should get out of here," Milos said.

They had snuck down into the cellar. They had done magic inside the palace. They had created an incredible pillar of fire like nothing he had ever seen before. Now all they needed to do was get out of there without getting caught.

They moved quickly towards the steep steps to the outside and scrambled up them. Milos extended his hands above him and pushed open the doors as he climbed. The room was again flooded with light from the sun, which hung almost directly overhead now.

He stepped up through the doors and held them open until Caleb climbed out past him. As soon as Caleb was clear of the doors, he closed them and secured them with the metal bar. They walked as quickly as he could, without seeming suspicious, towards the side door.

"Hold on a second," said Caleb from behind him. Milos stopped before the door and turned to watch Caleb hurry past him and back towards the carriage. He did not follow him this time. He watched from afar as Caleb removed the case and reopened its secret compartment.

Once the bottle of blue liquid was back in its hiding spot inside the carriage, Caleb casually walked back to Milos with a satisfied smile on his face. As far as Caleb was concerned, they were now in the clear, but Milos wanted to get back inside as soon as possible.

When Caleb was back beside him, he reached out and slowly opened the door. They both stepped through the door and found themselves face to face with Bina, who had just stepped out of the kitchen door holding a tray of food.

"Ah, so there you are Milos," she said. Milos froze in place, his heart suddenly racing. This was it, he thought, they were caught.

"Now where have you two been hiding?" asked Bina with a smile. Her eyes narrowed as she looked at Milos. His mind raced, but he could not think of what to say. She knew. She knew they were up to something. She was looking right through him.

When Milos did not say anything for an uncomfortably long time, Caleb spoke.

"Oh, Milos was just showing me around the grounds before lunch," he said smoothly as he looked down at her tray.

"How nice," said Bina as her eyes moved from Milos to Caleb's smiling face. Bina smiled back at him.

"Well, you are just in time. Everyone else has already been seated. Follow me," she said. She proceeded down the hall towards the dining room.

Milos trailed behind Caleb as he followed Bina down the corridor. He was sure Bina would press them for information, not let up until they confessed what they had done. But Caleb had diverted her attention with ease. To Milos, that was as impressive as conjuring a pillar of blue fire.

Bina entered the dining hall and spoke to the room at large.

"Here they are at last," she said without stopping. She leaned over and sat the tray down near the head of the table where Lord Andrik sat. He was speaking with the Lady Keren who was seated to his right.

All Lady Keren's advisors were arranged along the right side of the table. Caleb walked along that side of the table and sat in the seat at the end of the row of people. Milos was about to follow him when he saw Dimas. He was seated on the left side of the table at the far end of a row of his father's people. So Milos turned and walked down the other side of the table and instead sat down in the seat next to Dimas.

# 6: Perfect Crime

Lord Andrik waited until his son was seated then rose to his feet.

"Now that we are all here we can begin. Let me offer a toast," he said raising his glass. Everyone else at the table raised their drinks as well.

"To the health and prosperity of our guests. May their time in our city be time well spent. May it mark the beginning of a great friendship between our cities". When Lord Andrik finished speaking, he brought his cup down to his mouth and drank from it. The others followed suit.

Once Milos had taken a drink from his cup, he set it back down on the table. The shock of running right into Bina was starting to wear off. For the first time since he had left the cellar, he began to relax. He looked up the table at his father who was now seated. Everything had gone as planned, just like

Caleb said it would. His father would never know what they had done.

Milos looked across the table at Caleb who was surveying the food on the table hungrily. Silver trays full of food like the one Bina had been carrying were laid out in front of everyone. There were several large platters filled with thick slices of roasted meats, cheeses, and fruit.

All the guests began to move food from the trays to their plates. Lady Karen reached out and picked up a large fruit with smooth red and purple skin.

"Did someone tell you how fond I am of nika, Andrik?" she asked as she examined the fruit.

"I'm afraid it is only a coincidence. We often eat nika in the palace at this time of year," Lord Andrik replied.

He smiled as he watched her bring the fruit up to her nose, testing it for ripeness.

Lady Keren tapped the fruit on the table lightly until it split in half, revealing the soft yellow inside.

"I tried to grow them in Breen once. Unfortunately, they do not grow well so far from the river," she said setting the two halves down on her plate.

"Well, as you are so fond of them, I'm sure we can arrange to send some with you when you leave," said Lord Andrik.

"I would like that very much Andrik," she replied with a wry smile that reminded Milos of her son Caleb. Caleb had smiled just like that before conjuring the blue fire.

Milos was not sure what to think about Lady Keren. As far as he knew, she had never met his father before, yet she was being very familiar with him. She was not even bothering to use his title, which everyone in the palace always did. He watched as she picked up a spoon and began to eat the soft yellow fruit.

Milos also enjoyed nika, but he had never considered that its soft watery texture came from the water of the Dan River. He was reminded of what Dimas had said about the river the day before. About the flow of energy through the city. He pictured the river as it appeared on the maps in his room, a blue line arcing through the city. In his mind, the line glowed like the blue lines on the cellar floor.

Lord Andrik noticed the distracted look on his son's face.

"Milos, tell me what you and young master Caleb have been up to all morning," Andrik asked loudly. Milos jerked his head toward his father and was surprised to see him looking right at him.

"Oh," Milos began distractedly, "we, uh, we were in the palace."

Andrik raised his eyebrows expectantly but did not say anything. This time, Caleb did not wait for the uncomfortable silence to interject.

"Milos was showing me some of his books," he said with a pleasant smile.

Milos's head now jerked back towards Caleb. Was he going to tell his father about his secret books?

"You have a beautiful library, Lord Andrik," Caleb added, and Milos relaxed again. No, of course, he would not tell him. Now Milos felt a pang of shame for even thinking that Caleb would reveal his secret.

"Thank you, master Caleb," Lord Andrik said returning Caleb's warm smile. He turned back to

Lady Karen.

"I should have known. Milos is quite fond of books. It won't be too long before he's read the entire library."

Lady Keren finished another spoonful of nika.

"There are far worse things for a boy to spend his time on," she said, "especially one who must govern a city one day." Keren looked over towards Milos and then towards Caleb. Caleb met his mother's gaze for a moment and then returned his attention to his plate. Lady Karen helped herself to another spoonful of the yellow fruit.

When she had finished with her fruit, most everyone else appeared to be finished with their food as well. Lady Keren turned towards Lord Andrik.

"Thank you, Andrik, for your gracious hospitality," she said as she dabbed the corner of her mouth with her napkin. "I look forward to continuing our discussion tomorrow."

"Are you sure I cannot persuade you to stay with us here in the palace? We have more than enough room for you all," Andrik said with a gesture towards the people lined up beside Karen.

"That is very kind of you Andrik, but as I said before, we have already made other arrangements. We have many people to meet with, and we will only be able to stay in your city for a few days."

"In fact, I'm afraid it is time to take our leave of you," she said standing up. Andrik gave her a disappointed look, and she added "for now" with an indulgent smile. Milos again wondered whether his father had met Lady Keren before. They were acting like they knew each other well.

"Then allow me to escort you out," Andrik said rising to his feet as well. Everyone got out of their seats and followed Andrik and Keren out of the room in two neat rows. It was unusually orderly. This struck Milos as funny for some reason. Everyone was still on their best behavior.

Milos and Caleb took up the rear of each line, with Milos standing behind Dimas.

"So, you'll be returning tomorrow?" Milos asked excitedly turning to Caleb

"I guess so," he replied flatly.

The excitement Caleb had shown after they left the cellar was apparently gone. Caleb had reverted back to the same bored demeanor he showed when they first met.

When Lord Andrik and Lady Keren reached the front doors of the palace, they spoke briefly. Milos was too far back to hear them, but he saw his father stoop to kiss Lady Keren's hand. She walked out the doors, and the train of advisors followed her out with Caleb at the rear.

Once Andrik was satisfied that he had waited long enough to be polite, he slowly pushed the heavy doors shut. With all the guest now gone, everyone in the entry hall relaxed. Several people began to exchange quick words, but then stopped when they saw Lord Andrik wanted to address everyone again.

"That went pretty well," he said to the group. There was a murmur of agreement. "Lady Keren was very cordial, more than we expected at any rate. I think this bodes well for us," he added. Milos was confused by this. Did they expect their guests to be unfriendly? If anything, Lady Keren had been just the opposite

Lord Andrik turned to one of the advisors nearest him. They began to discuss their plans for tomorrow's meeting. Some of the others joined in, while the rest broke off into other small groups to consider what had happened that day. As his presence no longer seemed to be required, Milos made a discrete exit up the stairs and headed back towards his bedroom.

# 7: Sparked Ambition

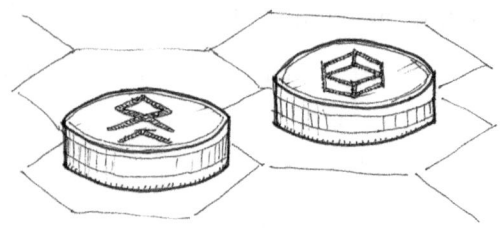

Milos turned the corner at the top of the stairs. The voices from the entry hall below became muffled and distant as he made his way down the corridor. He took a deep breath as he walked. He had forgotten how stressful it was to play the role of the noble son for guests. It was exhausting even when he wasn't concealing illegal magic he had performed in the dark cellar.

He opened the door to his room and stepped inside. He closed the door behind him and his eyes fell on the desk across the room. He froze with his back against the door. Two old and worn books were sitting there in plain sight. The smaller one was open to a page covered with a familiar circular pattern.

Milos usually did not risk removing the books from their hiding place unless it was late at night and everyone else was asleep. Then he could study them by the lamplight without getting caught. They looked unnatural and dangerous bathed in the sunlight from the window. He bound across the room and grabbed the books. He took one last look at the open page before snapping the book shut.

When the books were once again hidden in the box under his bed, he climbed on top of it and collapsed onto his back. He took another deep breath, and it occurred to him how careless he had been all day. Showing a boy he barely knew his secret books, leaving them out where anyone could find them.

He was so eager to prove he wasn't afraid, so eager to see magic. He had been so foolish. Even this morning, he had shown up to greet their guests with milk on his face. He had been so impatient to meet the boy Dimas told him about. The dark-haired boy. The boy who could do magic. A smile spread across his face as he again thought about the pillar of blue fire.

He closed his eyes and remember the scene in the cellar. The way it had writhed and pulsated as though it were alive, like no fire he had ever seen.

But if it was not fire, then what was it? It had only been an hour ago, but already he longed to see it again and study it more closely.

Gradually he opened his eyes again. Sunlight was still pouring through the open window onto the desk. He sat up and saw the books and maps he had roughly pushed aside that morning. The ones Dimas had left behind. He rolled out of his bed and walked over to his desk.

Milos grabbed one of the large maps and unrolled it in front of him. As he expected, it was a map of the whole region of Anadel. The map had been rolled tightly and kept trying to roll itself back up again. He grabbed a few of the books and set one at each corner of the map to hold it flat.

Milos scanned the map and immediately saw what he was looking for, the Dan River. He knew it did not matter which of the maps he unrolled, every one of them would have the river right through the center. If Anadel was a tree, then the river was its trunk. Everything branched out from a point along its gradual arc.

Milos dragged his finger along the map, tracing the river's path as it entered the city from the north.

It passed close by the palace before continuing out of the city towards the south. Milos sat down on the desk chair and stared at the map. He hoped that some pattern would emerge from the lines on the yellowing parchment.

Milos was thinking about what Dimas had said about the flow of the river through the city when there was a knock on his door. Without waiting for an answer, Dimas opened the door and stepped into the room. A smile crept upon his face as he saw Milos contemplating the old map.

"Surveying your lands my lord?" Dimas teased.

"You were the one who told me to study these maps" Milos replied.

Dimas's expression relaxed, but the smile remained.

"I just thought Lady Keren's comment might have sparked your ambitions," Dimas said.

Milos remembered about Lady Keren had said about Milos having to govern one day. Something he didn't think about very often. He remembered how she had glanced at him briefly before her eyes lingered on her own son.

"I think she was talking about Caleb, not me," Milos said.

Dimas's eyebrows raised as he crossed the room.

"That's very astute Milos, I quite agree," he said clearly impressed, "In fact, that is what I wanted to speak to you about."

Dimas grabbed a chair from along the wall and pulled it close to Milos. He sat down so that they were almost eye to eye.

"Your father and I spent all morning with Lady Keren and her company, but we hadn't given the boy much thought," he began. Now his smile was gone, and his tone was serious.

Dimas paused for a second, studying Milos.

"What did you think of Caleb?" he asked.

"Oh, he's okay I guess," Milos replied.

"What did the two of you talk about?"

"Well, he didn't talk very much, to be honest."

This was true enough. The trouble was, Caleb didn't say much until the subject of magic had come up, and Milos was keen to avoid that subject. Dimas did not usually pry the way Old Bina did, but still, he did not want anything to slip about what they had been up to.

"We played a game of padat," Milos said suddenly, hoping to steer the conversation in another direction.

"Is that so? I trust you won?" Dimas asked.

"Yes, I did... but I don't think he cares much for padat."

"What makes you say that?"

"He said padat is a stupid game."

"I bet he didn't say that until after you beat him"

Dimas was smiling again. Milos did not reply, but his own smile confirmed Dimas's guess.

"A sore loser. That is indeed a poor quality in a leader," said Dimas returning to a more serious tone.

"At any rate, your father will be pleased to hear you represented your family well on the padat board. Some people still put stock in one's skill at the game."

Milos beamed back at his teacher.

"Maybe one day I will be as good as you," Milos

said, hoping to sound modest.

"You've already beaten me several times, and I have been playing a lot longer than you," Dimas replied.

"If you keep practicing you will be better than me in no time. But as you saw today, not everyone thinks it is worth their time." Dimas let out a sigh.

"And it seems," he continued, "that we are not worth their time either. Apparently Lady Keren had more important things to attend to this afternoon."

"You mean you didn't know they would be leaving?" Milos asked.

"Not until Lady Keren told us this morning. Very unusual..."

Dimas paused for a moment, apparently considering the situation. Dimas spoke again, more quietly than before.

"Our guests are due to return tomorrow afternoon. That means you will have another opportunity to spend time with Caleb. See if you can't get our guest to speak more freely."

Milos frowned slightly.

"You want me to spy on him?" Milos asked.

"Not spy," Dimas said quickly, "and do not pry either. You don't want him to distrust you. I'm simply asking you to keep your ears open. Most likely you won't hear anything of importance, but your father thinks it might be worth trying all the same."

Milos turned back towards the map beside him. His eyes lingered on the footprint of the palace hatched with black ink. He nodded his head to show his agreement but did not respond.

"Good," Dimas said, returning to his feet. He pushed the chair back against the wall.

Dimas was about to turn and leave when Milos finally spoke.

"Dimas?" Milos asked tentatively.

"Yes, Milos?"

"If Caleb isn't staying with us here in the palace, where is he staying?"

Dimas took a step forward to look at the map with Milos. He placed his finger on an L-shaped building by the river, south of the palace.

"Lady Keren and Caleb are staying here, at the Karpat," Dimas said.

When Milos gave him a questioning look, he continued.

"The Karpat is owned by one of the wealthiest merchants in the city," Dimas said.

He gave Milos a meaningful look.

"This particular merchant has made much of his fortune trading with the city of Breen."

Milos looked back at the L-shaped building on the map.

"Well, I will see you tomorrow then," Dimas said after a few moments. "We will likely be working through dinner to prepare for the Lady Karen's return."

Dimas turned on his heel and walked out of Milos's room, pulling the door shut behind him.

# 8: Missing Something

Milos returned his attention to the map on his desk. Again he dragged his fingertip across it, following the path of the river. Into the city. Past the palace. As his finger touched the Karpat, he stopped. He slid his hand to the side and examined the little L-shaped footprint. He wondered if Caleb and Keren were already there or if they had gone somewhere else first.

Milos reached towards the end of the desk and grabbed a smaller map. When unrolled, this map showed the whole city, but at a larger scale. He could see the courtyard that wrapped around the palace and the road leading out of it.

As it wound down the hill the road branched off into more paths and intersected others that made their way around and over the rolling hills. The widest street made its way toward the river and the wide bridge across the River Dan.

A road near the bridge turned and ran parallel to the river. He traced this path with his finger until it came to a sudden end, fitting neatly into the crook of the L-shaped Karpat. Milos thought about Caleb, his face illuminated with sharp blue light. The light from the spell.

He pulled open one of the deep drawers of his desk and pulled out a piece of thick paper. He set the sheet down on top of the two maps and then began searching through another drawer. He brushed aside a few quills and pens and grabbed a stick of charcoal wrapped in wax paper. The paper was peeled back at the end, revealing the tip of the charcoal. He used it to draw a thick black line down the center of the sheet.

He drew more lines, trying to remember the exact order and pattern he had watched Caleb draw. When he finished with a full circle around the edges, he picked up the paper and examined it. Was that right? Milos hesitated for a moment, then rushed over to his bedside. With the drawing still in one hand, he reached under his bed with the other and pulled out the old box.

Crouched beside his bed, he flipped through the pages of his book. He quickly found the symbol he was trying to recreate. He held the drawing next to the book and compared them. Something was not quite right. Milos peaked over the top of his bed to make sure the door was still closed. He hurried back to his desk and set the book and drawing down on it.

He pulled a stack of the paper from his desk drawer and started again. This time, with the book as a reference, he was able to draw it almost perfectly. He repeated the process several more times, trying to refer to the page less each time. Eventually, he closed the book and drew it one last time with a sure hand.

Milos did not reopen the book to check, he knew he had done it correctly. He held up the paper and admired his work for a few moments. Then he let it fall back to the desk. The rush of excitement was already wearing off. He could draw the shape with charcoal, but what good was that? He already had a copy of it in his book. If he ever wanted to perform the spell, what he needed was that blue stuff, whatever it was.

Milos had never even heard of anything like it.

If it was used for magic, there was no way Dimas would have taught him about it. Whenever he tried to talk about magic, Dimas would always change the subject. He was pretty sure his father had told Dimas not to teach him about magic. He had learned long ago not to ask his father about it.

Milos picked up the book of spells and rifled through the pages half-heartedly. He knew he would not find any answers there. He must have looked through it a hundred times since he had swiped it from the library's musty storage room. If the other book under his bed said anything about it, Milos had no hope of reading or understanding it.

Both the books were a mystery themselves. The library was purged of books about magic a long time ago. Yet these books had been tucked away in a locked drawer in the storage room. It's possible that they had merely been missed during the purge. Nobody seemed to have noticed when they went missing from the storage room after he had decided to practice some lock-picking.

Milos gathered up all the paper he had used and put it into a neat stack, tapping the edge of the sheets on his desk. Then he placed them inside the old box underneath the books. After hiding the box under his bed, he returned to his desk and stood next to it. His closed fists rested on his hips as he looked down at the map of the city. Dimas would have laughed to see him standing there, surveying his lands.

Finally, Milos came to a decision. He looked through the books Dimas had brought him, they all had something to do with Anadel. Eventually, he found one that looked promising. It was holding down the northwest corner of his map. The corner curled up as Milos lifted the large book and read the cover. The words "Architecture of Anadel" were written in embossed gold letters across the blue cloth cover.

Milos flipped through the pages, looking for drawings of large buildings. Most of the significant structures in Anadel were shown in detail. Sure enough, Milos found a plan of a sizable L-shaped building with the word "Karpat" written under it. Milos hesitated only a moment before ripping the page out of the book.

He folded the page in half neatly, then once again so that it was small enough to slide into his pocket.

He closed the book and set it down on the map, forcing it to lay flat against his desk again. He took a step back, moving away from the light that was inching further into the room as the sun sank lower outside his window.

Milos left his room and walked down the wide main stair into the entry hall. Then he turned back up the north corridor towards the library. It would have been faster to go down the stairs he and Caleb had used that morning, but he knew the entrance hall would be empty with everyone huddled into his father's study. Everyone but the palace staff who would be busy around the kitchens.

Milos slipped into the library and stopped tentatively in the center of the tall room. He began to turn slowly on the spot. As his eyes slid across the bookshelves, he mentally searched through all the books he had read. Nothing he could remember seemed likely to contain information about the blue liquid.

He thought of searching the storage room again. It was through a small door in the corner of the room. Instead he continued onward into the reading room. He was resigned to the fact that he was unlikely to find anything new in a place he had search through so many times.

Milos walked over to a long padded bench by a window. He knelt down on the seat and rested his elbows on the window sill. He looked out across the city. At the foot of the hills, the river was glittering in the late afternoon sun. The glass of the windows beyond were squares of opaque white set in the pale stone walls.

In the whole city, there was only one place Milos knew he could find that blue liquid. If that's where he had to go, then that's where he would go.

# 9: PREPARATIONS

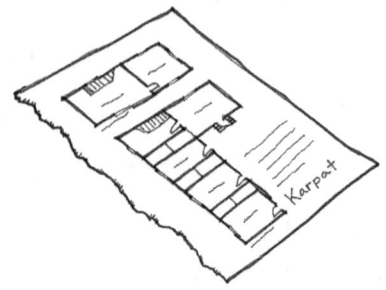

Milos stood up and reluctantly turned away from the window. He looked around and saw the padat table at the far end of the room. He walked over to it and saw the pieces were still in the final position from his game with Caleb. Dimas said that his father would be proud that he had won the game.

Milos opened the shallow drawer that sat flush with the side of the table. He brushed the padat pieces roughly into the drawer and pushed it closed again. Dimas also said not everyone cared about padat.

He sat down on one of the chairs and pulled the folded paper out of his pocket. He unfolded it and smoothed out the creases on the polished surface of the table. He studied the plan of the Karpat, trying to understand its layout.

Next to the L-shaped plan was another

rectangular plan. At first, he thought that this must be another building. Then he realized that it was a plan of the second floor. The shorter wing of the building must be taller than the rest of the building.

Some of the larger rooms were labeled, but most of them were not. The longer wing was divided into smaller rooms that he thought might be rooms for guests. He remembered from the map upstairs that this wing ran parallel to the river. All those windows on the east side must overlook the water.

Milos continued to study the layout of the building, trying to commit it to memory. The light of the day began to fade, and the room grew darker. He hunched forward to get closer to the paper. It wasn't until he became uncomfortable that he realized how dark it had become. It must be almost dinner time now.

Milos folded the page again and put it back in his pocket. He took one last look out of the windows as he walked back towards the door. Many of the windows across the river were still glowing. Now from lamps or candles burning inside the buildings rather than from the reflection of the sun.

Milos turned out of the reading room and

crossed the library into the corridor on the far side. As he stepped out into the hallway one of the house staff walked by him carrying a silver tray. They must be taking dinner to his father's study. Dimas had been right when he guessed they would be working late.

Milos turned towards the kitchen, relieved that he would not need to sit through another formal meal. When he reached the long wooden table outside the kitchen door, he saw that there was nothing on it to eat. He did not feel like sitting and waiting to be served, so he pushed the kitchen door open and stepped inside.

The room had an unnatural stillness that suggested that the room had recently been full of frantic activity. Now there were only two people left inside the kitchen. As soon as Milos was clear of the door, someone carrying a silver tray shuffled passed him and out of the kitchen. Only Milos and Old Bina stood in the quiet kitchen.

"Ah, Milos, did you think we had forgotten about you?" Bina asked.

Before he could answer, Bina turned and picked up a bowl and walked over to a large pot. She grabbed the metal handle that was sticking out of it and gave the contents a quick stir before lifting the ladle and pouring a steaming stew into the bowl.

Milos guessed that the stew had been made from all the leftover meat from lunch. Still, it smelled good all the same. Bina set a spoon into the bowl and walked over to Milos. She extended the bowl to him with a grin. As he took the stew, he glanced over Bina's shoulder at the door on the far side of the kitchen. The entrance to the cellar.

"Go on now and eat it while it's still hot," Bina said, returning Milos's attention to the bowl in his hands. He made no move to either leave or lift his spoon.

"Is everything alright, my boy?" Bina asked. Bina had always referred to him this way. Milos did not like it, but Bina did not care. Ever since Milos's mother had passed away, she felt a certain responsibility for him.

Milos looked up at Bina as if he had just noticed she was there. He stared at her for a few moments, then finally he spoke.

"Bina, have you ever been outside of Anadel?" he

asked

"Oh yes, but its been ages now," she replied.

"Have you ever been to Breen?"

"I've not been so far, but one place is much the same as another as I see it," Bina paused for a moment. "Why do you ask?"

"Oh, I was just thinking about our guests. I wondered what it's like outside the city, you know, where people can do magic."

"Oh it's not so different as you might think," Bina said with a chuckle. " You don't see people casting spells all over the place. You see a few trinkets around, but most people can't afford to cast spells every day. Magic's not cheap you know."

This had never occurred to Milos. He had imagined the lands beyond Anadel to be filled with wonders, especially after seeing the spell in the cellar beyond the door.

"Thank you, Bina," Milos said. Then he turned and walked back out of the kitchen.

Milos did not stop at the wooden table outside the kitchen door. Instead, he continued to the stairs and carried his dinner up to his room. He climbed onto his bed and began to eat absentmindedly. He knew that there was no rush, but he found it hard to pace himself. He was eager to get started. He did not realize that he had finished the stew until he heard the sound of his spoon scraping the bottom of the bowl. The noise brought his attention back to the present.

He set the empty bowl on his end table, slid off the bed, and walked over to the window. The sun was now completely behind the mountains to the west. The sky was fading from a deep purple to an inky black. A few of the brightest stars were already visible hanging above the ridges of the mountains. As he watched, a few more faded into view.

Milos guessed it would be at least another hour before he could sneak out of the palace unnoticed. He turned back to his desk and the map of the city. He considered the routes he might travel from the palace to the Karpat. He tried to commit these to memory as well. He had snuck out before, but he had never gone so far from the palace, nor so close to the river. He usually preferred to explore to the west of the palace. It was mostly open fields and large estates that way. There were few people who might see him.

Milos was starting to get nervous and found himself pacing around his room. He caught sight of himself in the mirror. He was still wearing the brightly colored shirt he had put on that morning. That would not do at all. Milos went back to his closet.

He tossed the yellow shirt and white pants into the corner, and searched for the darkest clothes he could find. He found a pair of long black pants and a dark blue tunic that was a bit tight. He could not remember the last time he had worn it. Milos walked over to his mirror to see how he looked. It would not win him any points for style, but he thought it would work well for moving unnoticed through the night.

He returned to his desk and pulled open the center drawer. He bent his elbow to reach all the way to the back of the drawer. He closed his hand around a cold, smooth object and pulled it up and out of the drawer. He held it up for a moment, examining the pearlescent handle of the folding knife. He unfolded the blade from the handle in a smooth motion. The knife appeared brand new. It had been used for little more than hacking away at some old wooden toys when Milos had gotten bored one day. Since then it sat unused in his desk drawer.

He pressed a button at the top of the handle with his thumb, which allowed him to fold the knife back into place. Folded in half, the knife was barely six inches long. He slid it into his pocket and walked over to his bedroom door and pressed his ear up against it. After he heard nothing for several minutes, he carefully pushed the door open and left his room.

# 10: PALACE KEY

Milos looked down the long hallway. It was sparsely lit with lamps alternating along each wall. The circles of light on the floor left a long serpentine shadow extending down the hall. The shadow seemed to writhe on the floor as the lamp flames flickered with each draft. Apart from this, there was no movement in the empty hallway.

Once he was convinced the hallway was deserted, he rushed on tiptoe to the north stairs. He paused for a moment at the top. Crossing the hall was the first obstacle. Now he was concealed from anyone who might look down the hallway at the wrong time. Milos crept down the stairs, holding tight to the rail on the wall. The only light in the stairwell came from high above the landing halfway down the stairs. This made it hard to distinguish one step from another.

When he reached the landing, he stopped again to listen. The next flight of stairs let out directly into the main hallway, which was much more likely to be occupied. Worst of all, his path would lead him right by the kitchens again. Bina was usually gone and in bed by now. But Milos could not shake the feeling that Old Bina could always sense when he was up to something. He half expected to see her standing there with her arms crossed when he turned the corner.

When he finally did descend the last stair, he saw nothing but an empty hallway between him and the side door. Milos closed his eyes and took a deep breath. Opening his eyes, he set off on another tiptoe run towards the door. As soon as he reached it, he flipped the small lever that unlocked the door. He began to slowly turn the handle, trying to make as little noise as possible.

As he felt the latch release, he thought he heard some footsteps from the far end of the hallway. He did not look back as he pulled the door open just wide enough to slide through. Once he was outside he pushed the door shut as fast as he dared and reengaged the latch.

Milos considered leaving this side door unlocked so that he could sneak back in later. But what if someone noticed and locked it before he got back? No, it was better to get the key just in case. Milos had never been given a key to the palace. But, he had managed to get one a couple years ago from a drawer in his father's study.

At first, he had kept the key stashed in the box under his bed. The first time he had taken it with him out of the palace, he decided it would be better to hide it outside somewhere. Somewhere only he would know about.

He moved quickly past the door to the cellar and made his way to the back of the palace. Back from the corner of the palace, in the middle of the grounds, stood a large ancient beech tree. The pale bark of the thick limbs twisted upwards with many shallow crooks and bends that started only a few feet from the ground. Milos had spent countless hours climbing this tree or slumped in the crook of the low branches reading a book.

Years ago, he got the idea that the old tree needed a birdhouse. Copying plans he had found in the library, he built a tall rectangular box with

74

a hole two-thirds of the way up the side. It was a kind of birdhouse made for red kites, a type of bird Milos later learned only lived on the other side of the country.

So the birdhouse hung empty on a branch of the beech tree, housing only the occasional spider until Milos had stashed the key inside it.

He bounded up the tree to the branch above the birdhouse. Then he lifted off its lid and reached in to retrieve the tarnished key. It was hanging on a wooden dowel that Milos assumed was supposed to be a perch for nesting birds. Now it had found a new purpose as a key hook.

Key in hand, he descended partway down the tree and then jumped down to the ground, crouching to muffle the sound. He ran back to the corner of the palace and then edged along the wall towards the front.

He stopped at the side door, locked it with the key, then stuffed the key into his pocket. He continued on towards the front of the palace, crouching down when he reached the front corner. This is where Lady Keren's carriage had been parked earlier that day. Inside that carriage was a leather satchel that held what Milos wanted.

If he was going to get it, he was going to have to go out into the city at night and make his way to the Karpat by the river. The prospect suddenly seemed terrifying. For a moment, he considered turning around and returning to his bed.

After all, Lady Keren was due to return tomorrow. Perhaps there would be an opportunity to grab one of the bottles without anyone noticing. Perhaps he could ask Caleb to give him one. Maybe Caleb would.

Milos sat crouched by the corner of the palace, not moving. As much as he wished he could be back in his bed, he could not bring himself to turn back. Thinking of Caleb reminded him of his conversation with Dimas earlier. Whatever Dimas said, it sure sounded like he wanted Milos to spy on their guests.

Milos's imagination began to run wild. What if he could return with more than just the bottle? What if he were able to get some critical piece of information that his father could use? He pictured an impressed look on his father's face as he presented some vital document to him. This idea filled him with resolve.

Maybe he wouldn't find anything useful, but surely it was his duty to try. That wasn't really true, but the idea gave him the courage and an excuse to press on. He would go to the Karpat, and if nothing else, he would return with a bottle of blue liquid.

For a fleeting moment, he considered the idea that stealing from Lady Keren was wrong. Stealing generally was. But he had an answer for this too. For one thing, the stuff was illegal. By bringing it into the city, he felt she had forfeited any claim to it. And besides that, Caleb had no problem taking some. Why couldn't he?

Still crouching, he began to move across the courtyard. Not straight towards the front gate, but towards the outer wall to his left. There was a low berm that ran between the palace and the outer wall on the north side. Once Milos was on the other side of it, he could stay hidden as long as he kept low.

He turned back towards the east and made his way to the front wall of the grounds. This corner was Milos preferred way out of the castle. It was far from the front gate and the guardhouse next to it.

Several of the rough cut stones protruded just enough for Milos to get the tip of his foot on them.

With a running start, he could kick off against the two walls and get high enough to throw one arm over the top of the wall.

Once his right arm was hooked over the top of the wall, he swung himself up on top. Then he turned again and let his legs drop down the outside of the wall. He worked his way down as far as he could, and then dropped the remaining few feet.

He had intended to soften his landing by crouching low again. But his foot slipped and he ended up falling backward and had to catch himself with his elbows. Once he had scrambled back to his feet, he was standing between the outside wall and the row of tall hedges outside the palace grounds.

# 11: Black Cat

Outside the walls, it was almost too dark to see. It was a cloudless night, and the sky was filled to the brim with stars. The waning moon was just beginning to rise, but it wouldn't provide much light to see by. Further down the wall, Milos could see the warm glow of the lamps by the front gate.

He began to make his way towards the end of the wall of hedges. He looked around the side of the last hedge and saw the broad stone road. It fell away from the palace entrance as it descended the hill.

This road wound down to the river and was lit intermittently with lamps all the way to the bridge. Milos would have to cross it at some point. Preferably far away enough from the front gate to avoid being seen by the guard.

At the top of the hill, the buildings were spaced apart from each other. Further down the hill, the buildings were built right on top of each other, their facades forming an unbroken wall apart from the occasional narrow alleyway.

Milos moved around the hedge and began to move away from the palace entrance. He was walking alongside a wide back street. On the other side of the street was another wall of neatly trimmed hedges. He could barely see them. Unlike the main road, this street had no lamps to light the way.

He made his way to a significant gap in the hedges across the street. The hedge on this side of the road was lower, and behind it were the stone walls of buildings. Moving through the gap, he started down another back road. Now he was walking downhill and away from the palace.

As the street wound down the hill, Milos was flanked closely by the backs of buildings on either side. Occasionally, a wide space would open up on one side or the other, revealing a private garden or stone court filled with carriages. Between the buildings, he could still see the main road. It appeared to glow in the dark night. But as he moved further down the hill, these glimpses of the main street were narrower and came less often.

Eventually, he found himself walking down a narrow dark street without gardens or alleys to the main road. Without warning, the street ended, dying into a dark cross street. Peering around the corner to his right, he could see the intersection at the main road. A man was standing on the corner closest to Milos so that he was silhouetted by the street lamps.

Milos froze and watched the man. After a minute the man turned and walked up the hill and out of sight. Milos turned to his left and moved away from the main road. He was hoping to find a more private path toward the river.

After a few yards, an alley appeared on his right, and Milos turned down it. Milos had only gone halfway down the alley before he encountered a massive iron gate that blocked his path. Milos examined the gate as best as he could in the dark. It was sealed with a thick bolt which was secured with a heavy padlock.

Moving through the interior courtyards would not be as easy as Milos had hoped. With exasperation, he left the alley and walked back towards the main road. As he reached the intersection, he kept tight to the wall.

He extended his head around the corner enough to see up the road. He wanted to make sure the man was not looking back down the hill before he crossed the street. The man must have already moved beyond the curve of the road because Milos could not see anyone.

He drew his head back behind the wall and turned to lean against it. Looking down the road in the other direction, he saw a man was walking up the other side and was almost to the intersection. In a panic, he stumbled backward, trying to get out of the light.

He started to fall and turned his body, landing on his knee before bouncing back to his feet. He ran as fast as he could, ignoring the pain in his knee. He did not look back until he reached the little alley that lead to the iron gate. As he turned into the alley, he got another glimpse of the man, who was walking across the main road in his direction. The lamps illuminating his guards uniform.

Milos ran into the alley and all the way back to the gate. He huddled down beside it, trying to make himself as small as possible. He was out of breath, and his heart was pounding in his ears. He could not be sure if the guard had seen or heard him. Perhaps the guard was merely crossing the street as part of his usual patrol.

After a while, Milos thought that this must be the case because he could not hear anyone coming. Just as he was beginning to relax again, the throbbing in his ears was replaced by the steady sound of footsteps advancing down the side street.

Milos closed his eyes tight and tried to sit as still and silent as he could. The footsteps grew louder, and he hoped desperately that they would pass by the alley without stopping. As he sat motionlessly, he felt something press against his leg. He was too afraid to open his eyes at first, but then he heard an unmistakable sound right in front of him.

Milos opened his eyes to look down at a sleek black cat purring as it rubbed up against his leg. He did not move. The cat rubbed up against him again, but then froze and raised its head and ears up high. With a sudden intensity, the cat moved towards the side street with small crouching steps.

When the cat looked around the corner, it relaxed and walk casually out into the street. The cat stopped and let out a short inquisitive sounding meow.

"Pah! Another stupid cat!" a man's voice said from around the corner. There was a scraping sound, and Milos saw a heavy boot kick out towards the cat.

The cat jumped to the side, dodging the kick, and ran back to the iron gate. It slipped effortlessly between the bars, and a moment later it's black fur disappeared into the dark. The footsteps resumed. This time each step was quieter than the last as the guard moved away from the alley and back towards the main road.

It was long after the sound of footsteps had gone that Milos dared to move from his corner in the alley. That had been very close. If the guard had found him, he probably would have been dragged back up to the palace. He would have been forced to account for his late night escapades. Or worse, if the guard did not recognize Milos, who knows what he would have done with him.

Finally, he moved back into the side street, more cautiously than before. He slowly made his way back to the intersection. Only after checking and rechecking that no one was around, he sprinted across the main road. He did not stop until he was several buildings past the intersection, where all was dark again.

Milos was now across the main road and guessed that he was at least halfway to the Dan river now. The ground was more level here, the rolling hills tapering away as they neared the riverside. He continued towards the river. Whenever he was forced to deviate from his eastward path, he tended towards the south. This should bring him closer to the Karpat when he finally reached the river's edge.

Twice more he was forced to cross wide roads with flickering street lamps. The close call by the main road had inspired a great deal of patience in Milos. On both occasions, he crossed the streets only after waiting and watching until he was completely sure that no one would see him. After slowly making his way down the hill, he finally reached what he had been looking for.

# 12: THE KARPAT

Milos looked across another wide road lit with street lamps. But there were no streets on the other side. Instead, a row of large buildings obscured the river beyond. There were large gaps between most of these buildings, but it was too dark to see the water from across the road.

Still, there was no mistaking that the river was there. Milos could hear the running water. It was much quieter then he imagined it would be up close. It was a low rushing sound accompanied by the tinkling sound of water tumbling over rocks and sand.

The presence of the river was far more apparent due to the smell which filled the air. Milos realized that the scent had been growing steadily as he moved closer to it. It was not an unpleasant smell. It was not a particularly pleasant smell. But it was

86

a strong smell, which seemed palpable in the air. He licked his lips subconsciously. He was sure he could taste the air here. It was not unlike Old Bina's cabbage stew.

He watched to make sure no one was watching. After using up all the patience he had left, Milos dashed across the street. He ducked between two large buildings. The sides of each building contain large wooden doors which he guessed lead into storerooms.

The cobblestone path between the buildings abruptly changed. Milos was now walking on wood planks which sloped downwards. The planks were suspended over the flowing water on numerous posts driven into the riverbed. He went to the edge of the dock to take a closer look at the river.

The sounds of the water were joined by the buzzing and chirping of insects which seemed to emanate from everywhere. The surface of the water rippled slightly, which made the reflections of the stars dance. The quarter moon was high now, and in the mirror of the river, it seemed to wave like a flag in a soft breeze.

A loud chirp above him cause Milos to look up

in time to see a small dark shape swoop by. Milos thought it was some kind of bird, but then he realized it must have been a bat, hunting insects by the water. He turned away from the river and walked back up to the cobblestone path which was several feet above the water.

Milos moved south along the riverside. The wide spaces between the buildings gave him regular views of the road which curved with the river, just as it had appeared to on the map. Many windows were facing out over the water, but almost all of them were dark.

Up ahead, he saw a conspicuously tall building over the tops of the nearby roofs. Several large windows on the second floor were still lit with a warm glow. When he got closer, he also saw a long, low wing extending towards him from the building.

The lower part had several windows overlooking the river. Milos reached into his pocket to retrieve the drawing of the Karpat. It was not there. He closed his eyes in frustration as he remembered changing pants before leaving the palace. He had forgotten to remove the folded page from his pocket before tossing his old pants aside.

Still, he was sure that this was the right place. He reached the corner of the low wing and ducked into the alley that led back to the road. From the alley, Milos could see where the road died into a dimly lit courtyard in front of a large L-shaped building.

On the far side of the courtyard, there was a large pair of ornate doors with an arched top set above wide stone steps. Polished brass letters were nailed above the doors. He could read them even though it was so dark because he already knew what they said. Karpat.

Milos scanned the courtyard. It was surrounded by a low wall, no higher than his waist. In the center of the yard was a round pool of water. On the far side of it, two carriages were parked one behind the other. He could not tell which carriage belonged to Lady Keren from here. They looked identical in the dark.

He stepped over the low wall before skirting around the outside edge of the courtyard. He stopped when the carriages were between him and the front door of the Karpat. Then he made his way over to the first carriage and knelt down next to it.

As well as Milos could remember, this was just like the carriage that was parked by the front of the palace earlier that day. It had a door to a luggage compartment near the front just like the one Caleb had opened to retrieve the leather case.

He unlatched the compartment door and pulled it open. The compartment was lined on the bottom and sides with thick felt. He noticed several scrapes and marks on the felt. These were easy enough to see as the compartment was completely empty. He pushed the door shut again and re-latched it. He shifted over to the second carriage.

Before he even opened the luggage compartment, he knew the case would not be inside. This carriage was similar to the first, but not exactly the same. The side door was a little narrower, and the spoked rear wheels were larger. He opened the luggage compartment anyway to be sure. This compartment was just as empty as the first, though it was slightly more squat in proportion.

Milos stuck his head around the side of the carriage and looked up at the windows on the second floor. There was still a warm glow inside. Occasionally a shadow would cross the window as if people were walking around the source of the light, but he could not hear any voices.

He looked over at the low wing of the building. It was lined with doors and square windows. They were all dark. He made his way over to the side of the building and began to look through the windows. Some of them were covered from the inside by curtains. Through the ones that were not, he could see identical rooms, each with a bed set against the south wall.

Even though it was very late at night, the beds were empty. This was surprising as the rooms appeared to contain the missing contents of the luggage compartments. The leather case, however, was not among the bags he could see through the windows. Either it was in one of the rooms with the curtains drawn, or else it was upstairs where the lamps were lit. If it was the latter, he had no hope of getting to it tonight.

He took a last look up at the light from the windows above. Then he stepped back over the low wall and made his way back behind the building. Moving along the river, he started to look into the windows that overlooked the water. The windows facing the river were much larger. This gave him a clear view of the same identical rooms from the other direction.

Not all the rooms were unoccupied. Someone was sleeping in one of the beds. The room was dark, but based on the size of the lump in the blanket, it was not an adult. It must be Caleb. It seemed he was the only person from Breen who was not attending the meeting upstairs.

It was not surprising that he was asleep though. Milos had completely lost track of time, but he knew it was very late. Why was Lady Keren meeting so late? Who was she meeting? He pushed these questions out of his mind. After one last look into Caleb's room, he resumed his search.

Finally, he reached the window looking into the last bedroom. The curtains were drawn, but not entirely. There was a gap big enough for him to see the end of the bed. At the foot of the bed, he could see a neat row of luggage. Among them, leaned against the wooden foot board, was the leather case.

# 13: THE KNIFE

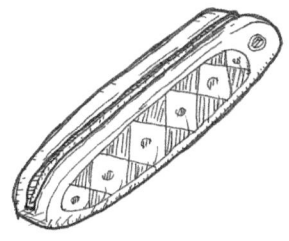

Milos tried to open the window into the bedroom, but it was either locked or sealed shut. He moved back to the courtyard, trying not to make too much noise in spite of his mounting excitement. He found the door into the room and pulled on the handle. The door would not budge. He moved to the small window next to it, but it did not look like it was made to open at all.

Milos took a step back and surveyed the door carefully. Below the fixed handle was a wide keyhole. He bent down next to it and tried to look inside the lock. To his surprise, he could see all the way through the keyhole to the room inside. It was an old fashion lock that could be locked or unlocked from either side with the same key. Some of the doors in the palace worked the same way, though none of them led outside.

He put one hand on the ground and leaned to his side. With his other hand, he reached into his pocket and produced the folded knife. He was grateful he had at least brought something useful, even if he had forgotten the building plan.

Looking down at it, Milos was filled with a mixture of excitement and anxiety. He carefully unfolded the knife with both hands, making sure not to cut himself. Then he leaned his shoulder against the frame of the door, bringing his eyes level with the keyhole again.

He inserted the tip of the knife into the keyhole and then angled it to the side. He felt for the locking mechanism inside. As he dragged the blade tip along the inside of the keyhole, he hoped he was not damaging the knife too severely. He felt several pieces of metal that moved when he pushed on them, pivoting up and away from the keyhole.

After poking at the keyhole for several minutes, he worked out that there was a metal cylinder in the lock. He also determined that he needed to turn the cylinder a full rotation to disengage the door latch. There was no way he was going to do it with a knife.

Milos did the only other thing he could think to

do and jammed his knife between the door and the frame. He crouched close to the door and pushed up on the knife handle as hard as he could. The latch held strong at first. Suddenly there was a low metallic click as the latch was forced up and out of the door frame.

He folded the knife back into its handle and returned it to his pocket. Then he reached out and pushed the wooden door, which swung into the dark room. Milos crept inside and pushed the door shut behind him. He thought to lock it before remembering that he had no way of re-locking it. The latch had rolled up into a pocket in the door. The only way he could extend it again was with the door's key.

Milos made his way over to the foot of the bed where the leather case sat. He grabbed the handle and swung it up onto the bed. He unbuckled the straps that held the case shut and lifted the lid. The case was still filled with all sorts of papers and notebooks. Maybe there was some useful information in here he could bring back. But instead of going through the documents, he curled his fingers up behind the lip of the case's lid.

He dragged his fingers from side to side until he felt a small protrusion behind the lining of the case. Milos pressed the hidden button. The top panel of the case fell forward onto the papers, revealing the secret compartment. Milos's eyes grew round with amazement.

The blue bottle that Caleb had shown Milos in the dark cellar had glowed in the dim light. But here in the dark room, the dozens of bottles gave off an intense light. He had the impression that he was staring into the face of the full moon, hanging only a few feet in front of him.

As his eyes adjusted to the bright glow, he could make out the small bottles. They were held in place by rows of leather loops that undulated across the back of the case. He reached out and pulled one of the bottles from its loop. He could see no markings on the bottle or on its plain cork stopper.

He stared transfixed at the luminous blue liquid. He tilted the bottle back and forth, watching the viscous stuff slide around the inside of it. Almost without thinking, he lowered his hand down to his side and put the bottle in his pocket. Then he looked back at the case. The spot where the bottle had been now looked like a dark hole surrounded by the other glowing bottles.

He thought for a moment about whether he should take another one. Maybe he should take them all. After all, this kind of stuff wasn't supposed to be in the city anyway. By his father's right, he could seize any magical items brought into the city illegally. Milos looked into the glowing case longingly.

But then he thought about Caleb. Milos assumed that even one missing bottle was not likely to go unnoticed. Lady Keren might think her son had taken it. After all, he had clearly used the stuff before. But what if all the bottles vanished? What would Lady Keren think then?

Caleb would have no reason to take the entire stash. But if someone had taken them all, then someone must have told them how to get it. Lady Keren could not report the theft to Milos's father, not without admitting she had brought the stuff into the city in the first place. So while Milos was unlikely to get into trouble himself, Caleb could end up in big trouble.

With a pang of disappointment, Milos lifted the

false panel up out of the case. He fixed it back in place over the secret compartment. It fit so snugly that none of the blue glow inside was detectable once it had clicked into place. He pulled the lid of the case closed and was about to re-fasten the straps. Then he hesitated.

Had he not resolved to find information for Dimas and his father? He had gotten what he came for, but there was something else he was supposed to do. He thought for a moment about trying to listen in on the meeting upstairs. No, that would be too risky.

But maybe there was some information here in Lady Keren's room. Milos began to open the case again to look through the documents inside. A sound outside caused him to freeze with the lid of the half-open case in his hand. A second later he was sure he had not imagined it. There were several pairs of footsteps growing louder outside in the courtyard.

He dropped the lid of the case and slid it off of the bed, letting it fall against the bed's foot board. He could hear hushed voices outside the door now. He dashed over to the large window overlooking the river. He searched frantically around the frame of the window. He found a brass rod holding the window shut on the bottom of one side.

He pulled the rod out of the frame and pushed on the window. It moved a bit, but it was still stuck on the other side. Milos heard the metallic sound of a key sliding into a lock behind him. Luckily, Lady Keren had not noticed that the door was already unlocked. He reached over to the other side of the window and pulled a second brass rod out of the frame.

Now when he pushed on the window, it swung up and out of the frame. He did not look back as he threw one leg over the window sill and then the other. He dropped down to the stone walkway, letting the window fall shut behind him. The ground outside was at least a foot lower than the floor of the room.

He could have sworn he heard the door of the room opening behind him as he had slid out of the window. But Milos did not wait to find out if someone had seen or heard the window falling shut. He turned to the north and began running along the river, away from the Karpat.

# 14: Trapped

Milos did not stop running until he could no longer see the high roof of the Karpat behind him. He paused a moment to catch his breath. His heart was racing. That had been a close call. His lungs were burning, but he knew he should not stop. He continued on in a fast walk along the river, looking for a good spot to cross the road.

He had not heard anyone following behind him as he ran, but he was gradually becoming aware of all the signs of his forced entry he had left behind. The unlocked door. The unlocked window. The unlatched case.

It would not take them long to figure out someone had been in Lady Keren's room. Milos needed to get far away from there as fast as he could. When he found a wide alley leading back to the road, he turned down it and stopped at the corner of the building.

He did not see anyone in either direction. After waiting for a far shorter time than he would have liked, he dashed across the street. He was sure that at any moment someone would come running up the road hoping to catch the intruder.

Once he was across the street, he continued on, doing his best to retrace his path down the hill in reverse. Milos was not too concerned about getting lost though. As long as he kept heading north and west, he would eventually encounter the main road.

He tried to keep moving quickly up the hill, but the streets of Anadel now seemed more occupied than they were when he had left the palace. He found himself having to avoid people. Some of them were guards, some of them were not. Occasionally a carriage would roll by with large suspended lamps illuminating the street.

At first, Milos did not understand what this meant, but it suddenly dawned on him as he turned onto a broad westbound street. This gave him a view of the mountains off in the distance. One of the highest peaks was reaching up towards the shining half moon. The moon appeared massive as it loomed above the jagged mountain peaks.

The mountains obscured the western horizon, so he could not be sure how much time he had. But he was confident that the sun would rise before the moon began to slide behind those peaks. It was no longer late at night, but early in the morning. Still very early in the morning, but all the same, much more time had passed than he had realized.

He began to run again, now it was a race against time. He needed to reach the palace before the first rays of sunlight. Otherwise, he was sure to be caught sneaking back to his room. The trouble was, the further up the hill he got, the busier the streets seemed to become.

Now he was encountering someone every few minutes. He only stopped long enough to make sure they were not guards patrolling the streets. They rarely were. The people of Anadel whose work required them to be up before dawn now outnumbered the guards on the roads. These people had no interest in Milos if they noticed him at all.

Finally, he came to the well lit main road. He waited for an opportunity to cross when no one was around. This seemed to be impossible. The streets might not be bustling with activity yet, but there always seemed to be at least one carriage or pedestrian in sight.

Milos was watching the road so intently, he did not notice the carriage coming up behind him, not until it was almost on top of him. The carriage passed by him without slowing down. On an impulse, he began to walk quickly beside the carriage. He stayed as close as he could as it crossed the main road.

He tried to walk as casually as possible, trying not to attract any attention. It was not until he reached the far side of the road that he realized he had been holding his breath the whole way across. He stopped holding his breath as he passed out of the street lights of the main road. He slowed down and let the carriage pull ahead of him, leaving him alone in the street.

Even though he was now out of the lamplight, the darkness did not seem to return as completely as before. Maybe it was just his imagination, but Milos was sure he could feel the impending sunrise coming as if were right behind him He turned up an alley halfway down the street and resumed his uphill run.

The hill got steeper as he moved up the street, but he also saw fewer people. He was back into the larger estates where most of the residents felt no compulsion to rise before the sun. This also meant that he was getting close to the palace.

He emerged onto a narrow street flanked by tall green hedges. Now there was no mistaking the pale orange color creeping into the deep blue of the sky. He was running out of time.

He rushed across the street and began skirting along the hedges. This brought him uncomfortably close to the palace's front gate as he reached the end of hedge. He quickly cut around it and moved back away from the gate through the space between the hedge and the palace wall.

Now all he had to do was get over the palace wall and sneak back into the side door. Unfortunately, getting over the wall from the outside was not as easy as it had been from the inside. The ground outside the wall was lower than the courtyard inside. Also, he could not push off against two walls as he had done on the interior corner.

Luckily, this was not his first foray outside the palace wall, and he knew the best place to get back in. He turned the corner and made his way along the north wall until he came to a familiar spot.

The stonework on this part of the wall was particularly rough. Even a few intrepid vines had noticed how easy the wall was to climb here. These vines thrived in the constant shade of the north wall. Several thin green tendrils wound their way halfway up the wall, sprouting angular clusters of leaves as they went. Milos began kicking at the base of the vines to clear them away, making sure to get them all.

They caused intense itching and swelling wherever their leaves brushed against bare skin. He had discovered this the hard way on a previous outing. It was not a mistake he intended to repeat, no matter how much of a rush he was in.

Once the wall was clear of vines, he began to climb. It usually took a few attempts to get all the way to the top, but this time it was especially tricky. He slid back down to the ground and crouched low, resting his legs. They felt weak and rubbery after his constant uphill run.

He took in a sharp breath through his nostrils and stood up straight again. He stepped back and looked at the wall and found that he could make out the footholds more clearly than usual. Then in a sudden shock, he realized this was because there was more light than usual. He usually had to climb the wall in the dead of night.

Milos began to climb again and progressed steadily until he was able to reach the top with one hand. Once he got a hold of the top with both hands, he swung his legs up as before, then dropped down on the other side of the wall.

He looked up towards the palace. It was silhouetted against a dimly lit pre-dawn sky. From where Milos had landed, his view of the side door was obscured by the low berm close to the palace wall. If he stood up, he would be able to see it, but instead, he decided to be cautious.

He crawled along the ground until the top of his head was level with the berm. Then he lifted his body slightly giving himself a brief glimpse of the side door. He immediately dropped back down flat against the ground, horrified at what he had seen. Two guards flanked either side of the door, keeping watch.

## 15: Distraction

He was so close to the safety of his room, but it made no difference if he could not actually get inside the palace. Milos started to panic a bit and tried to think of some way, any way of getting inside. The front door was no good. The key should unlock it, but he was sure to be seen going in that way.

There was another door on the south end of the palace, much like the one he had intended to use. Only it was on the completely wrong side of the building. Milos would have to cross the whole length of the palace to get to his room on the north end. This was assuming that door was not also blocked by guards.

He thought of getting in through the cellar and sneaking up through the kitchen. This plan had two major flaws. First, it was likely that some member of the staff was already in the kitchen, maybe even

Bina herself. Second, the door to the cellar was in plain view of the guards standing right across from him.

Milos stole another quick glance at the door over the top of the berm. The guards had not moved. He had not expected them to be posted there. During his previous excursions, a guard or two wereusually patrolling the grounds. They were easy to avoid since they moved steadily around holding up their oil lamps in the dark.

Milos had never returned so close to dawn. He guessed that with the growing light, the guards no longer felt the need to wander around with lamps. If he was right, they probably had no intention of moving until morning came. Then they could abandon their watch and go home.

He put his head into his hands, his panic steadily growing. He could not think of any way of getting into the palace apart from the side door. And he could not think of any way of getting past the guards.

Milos reached into his pockets desperately hoping to find something that could help him. One pocket contained only a folding knife and a key to the palace. He thought that maybe if he threw the knife to the side of the palace, he might distract the guards long enough for him to sneak through the door.

It seemed very unlikely that the guards would be fooled by such a stupid trick. In fact, they would probably see where the thing had been thrown from and walk straight over to his hiding spot. Milos reached into his other pocket. It contained nothing but a small glass bottle filled with glowing blue liquid.

Milos rolled over onto his back and pulled the bottle out of his pocket. He stared at the blue glow emanating from between his fingers which clutched the bottle tightly. The light seemed to have an immediate calming effect on him. The growing dread he had felt started to melt away, and in its place, a new plan began to form.

He could not fool the guards by throwing his knife, but maybe he could distract them another way. Distract them long enough for him to get to the door, unlock it, and slip inside before they returned.

He slid back down the side of the berm and found a patch of hard earth. He cleared away a few of the larger rocks and some scraggly plants until he was satisfied that the space was suitable.

Milos sat with his legs crossed in front of his freshly prepared canvas, then held the bottle up in front of his face again. He closed his eyes for a moment and remembered sitting at his desk with a piece of charcoal in his hand. He reached up and pulled the cork stopper from the neck of the bottle.

If he had misgivings before about performing magic in the palace, he felt none of them now. It could be because of his panic and fear of being caught outside, or maybe it was his fascination with magic and his deep longing to see the spell again. Perhaps the blue glow from the bottle was calming his fears. Soothing his nerves. The light was comforting to him.

Milos placed his index finger over the mouth of the bottle the same as he had seen Caleb do in the cellar. Turning the bottle over and back again, he deposited a blob of the blue liquid onto his fingertip. Then, reaching out across the clear space, he dragged his finger in a straight line across the ground.

Just as Caleb had, Milos repeated this process,

again and again, each time making a new glowing blue line on the ground. Milos felt sure that the order, direction, and proportions of the pattern were all critical to the spell working. This was why he had practiced drawing the spell until he could do it by heart.

He fell into a steady rhythm as he moved his hand between the ground and the bottle. There was something meditative about drawing the lines with his finger. He was completely relaxed now, in spite of the ever-growing light in the sky.

Milos made his final stroke, a full circle drawn counterclockwise, inscribing itself around the intricate geometry. His finger came to rest at the far end of the loop. He now noticed how much larger this circle was than the one Caleb had made in the cellar.

He held up the glass bottle and saw that it was already half empty. He had not intended to use so much of it. He moved to put the cork back into the bottle, but then remembered the final step of the spell. He turned the bottle over one last time, depositing more of the liquid on his finger. Then, he held his arm out over the center of the glowing pattern on the ground.

Milos took a deep breath and held it as he snapped his fingers, forcing a blue drop to fall from his fingertip. It seemed to fall in slow motion as his eyes followed it down to the center of the circle. He continued to hold his breath as nothing seemed to happen.

He finally exhaled as the burning in his chest grew uncomfortable. It was then that he noticed the blue lines on the ground began to glow more brightly. At first, he could only stare at the growing light in front of him. Wisps of smoke began to rise from the ground as dust and dirt were burned away by the now white hot lines.

His fixation on the spell was broken when he heard a guard speak loudly from near the side door. One of them had noticed the bright light illuminating the palace wall. All at once, the panic that had melted away returned to him in a crushing wave.

Fumbling with the bottle, he managed to get the cork back into place before returning it to his pocket. He turned away from the light and began to crawl as fast as he could. He needed to be far away from the spell before the guards came to investigate. Otherwise, his plan would backfire horribly, getting him into more trouble instead of getting him out of trouble.

Once he was almost to the corner of the palace wall, he turned and crawled to where he could see the side door again. The door was unguarded. He raised himself slightly to see where the guards were. They were moving toward a swirling pillar of glowing blue smoke. The guard nearest to it had drawn a short sword from his belt.

He watched them for a few seconds. Once he was convinced that their attention was focused entirely on the spell, he rose to his feet and ran to the corner of the palace. Once he reached it, he turned and moved towards the side door, behind the backs of the guards.

The guard nearest the growing pillar of smoke was looking up at it transfixed. The other guard stood further back and seemed to be trying to convince his fellow guard to move back.

Milos reached the side door and pulled the palace key from his pocket. He was about to insert the key into the lock when the air was filled with a deafening sound. It was as if someone had fired a hurricane out of a cannon. He knew what had made the sound. He wheeled around to see the flames, but what he saw filled him with terror rather than awe.

# 16: Flame and Fear

By the time Milos had turned around, the pillar of swirling blue flames already stretched up higher than the roof of the palace. His eyes were drawn up towards the top which grew wider and twisted more violently the higher he looked.

The courtyard was flooded with an intense blue light that gave everything a pale ghostly appearance. Where the sky had been growing gradually lighter, it now appeared dark again behind the massive pillar of fire.

The flames continued to grow. Now they dwarfed the old beech tree. Its thick branches appeared to shake and bend under the canopy of fire. Milos could feel gusts of hot air across his face as he looked up at the jagged flames at the peak. They reached up and up until Milos could no longer tell how big the fire was.

It loomed ominously above the palace, above the hills, above the whole city. He thought it must be as high as a mountain now. He had lost all sense of its scale. Even his sense of time seemed to have failed him, he felt trapped in a moment of terror. He felt like an ant looking up at a faceless giant that could crush him in a whim.

The flaming tower had become so vast at the top that it looked like a gigantic funnel. The massive head whipped around chaotically as it reached frantically towards the sky. If it grew any bigger, Milos feared it would collapse and fly apart, raining fire down upon the city.

The flames did seem to be flying apart at the wide brim. It was no longer a solid column of flame but was becoming like a tattered cuff. He was sure the flames were about to fall and cover the city in a ragged blanket of fire. The gaps in the fire only grew as the long fingers of flame began to dissipate.

From top to bottom, the pillar of fire became thin and feeble until it disappeared completely. What had a moment before been indescribably huge shrank with alarming speed. As if it were all being sucked into a small circle near the outer wall of the palace.

Then darkness and silence flooded the courtyard. The spell had been so loud and so bright, the stillness that followed it seemed just as deafening. Milos thought that he had been struck blind and deaf. But that notion was dispelled when he heard the cries of the guard.

He looked down at the ground between himself and the outer wall. One of the guards was kneeling over the other who lay motionless on his back. The first guard called out for help again as he hooked his arms underneath the arms of his partner on the ground. He began to drag him backwards towards the door where Milos stood.

Milos spun around and jammed the palace key into the lock. He unlocked the door and returned the key to his pocket as he pulled open the door. Once the door was open, he ran inside, pulling the door partially closed behind him. He dashed straight for the stairs by the kitchen without stopping to see if anyone else was in the hall.

Grabbing the handrail at the base of the steps he turned hard and bounded up the stairs, skipping as many as he could along the way. Once he reached the top of the stairs, he sprinted across the hall without stopping. He grabbed the handle of his bedroom door and yanked it open, stepped inside and pull the door shut again.

He stood breathing heavily for a minute. Without thinking, he locked the door behind him and walked in a daze into his room. He felt off balance, and when he reached his desk, he leaned against it with both hands.

He thought back on the rapid journey from the side door to his bedroom. He could not remember seeing anyone as he ran. When no one came knocking on his door, he felt sure he had made it back unseen. Under normal circumstances, he would have been proud of himself, but he was not.

Leaning against the desk, he closed his eyes. His mind was filled with visions of violent blue flames swirling all around him. He felt trapped by the fire. There was no way out. On the ground in front of him lay the figure of a man who looked like a ghost in the pale blue light.

Milos forced his eye open again. This proved harder than expected. Apart from shock and terror, he had spent the whole night running around the city. He had not slept, and he was exhausted. But he did not think he would be able to sleep. His mind was churning in a thick haze, and when he closed his eyes, all he saw was blue fire.

The spell that Caleb had shown him was like a child's toy in comparison to what he had just seen. The small pillar of fire in the cellar had seemed tame and beautiful. The gargantuan tower of flame in the courtyard had seemed uncontrollable and dangerous.

It had hurt at least one person. Milos hoped the guard was not too severely injured. He began to wonder if the guard would survive. Maybe he was already dead. He pushed this thought from his mind as best he could. He knew that whatever happened, it was his fault.

How could he have been so stupid? Performing a strange spell right in the palace grounds. He could not understand why it had seemed like such a good idea at the time. Thinking back on it now, it seemed crazy to even consider it.

He was pretty sure he had not made a mistake in performing the spell. What might have happened if he had? Maybe he would have blown up the whole palace. He never imagined the small bottle of blue liquid could conjure something so massive.

These thoughts raced through his head faster than he could process any of them. He let his head hang down and noticed with some surprise that the front of his shirt was covered with dirt. This reminded him of all the things he still needed to do.

He reached into his pocket and pulled out the folded knife. He pulled the blade from the handle and examined it. The tip and edge were bent and blunted. He refolded the mangled knife and returned it to the back of his desk drawer. He could probably get it repaired one day, once he thought of a good explanation for why it was so damaged.

He then removed the palace key from the same pocket. He had intended to return the key to its hiding place in the beech tree, but things had not gone according to plan. He would simply have to keep it hidden in his room for now. He walked over to his bed and once more retrieved the box from underneath it, setting it on his bed and opening the lid.

He looked down at the books and stacks of paper underneath them. Each page containing a drawing of the spell he had just performed. These were drawn with harmless black charcoal, not the dangerous blue liquid in his other pocket. Milos set the key down at the edge of the box and then hesitated for a moment. He reached into his pocket and pulled out the small glass bottle.

The bottle was half empty now, but the blue liquid still glowed brightly. It was dark in Milos's room, even though the sky was now a pale orange color. His room seemed eerily quiet for some reason. It took several minutes for Milos's groggy mind to work out why.

Even though the dawn had finally come, there were no birds out in the courtyard chirping and singing in the new day. He did not blame them. He wondered if they would ever return to the courtyard. He remembered reading that birds had long memories, that they could pass their knowledge down to their offspring through songs.

He stood lost in thought for several minutes. His mind returned to the bottle in his hand. He thought he might have fallen asleep for a moment. He could barely keep his eyes open. He put the bottle into the box and slid everything back under his bed. He pulled off his dirty clothes and tossed them aside. Then he lay down sideways across his bed and fell dead asleep, not remotely aware of the growing commotion downstairs.

# 17: Big Mistake

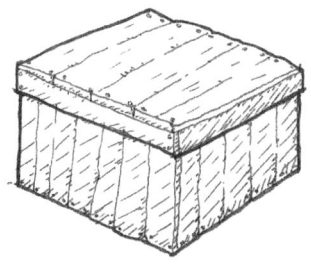

Milos was woken by a loud banging on his door. He had no idea how long he had been asleep. His mind was still numb and buzzing with incoherent thought. Someone was calling him. Then more banging on the door.

"I'm here," he called out blearily. He looked around his room. It was dark. Either he had slept into the evening or else it was still early morning.

"Milos, unlock the door!" called out the voice in an urgent tone. He pushed himself off the side of the bed until his feet touched the floor. Then he shuffled over to his door. Just as he had reached it, he heard Dimas shouting as he banged on the door again, "Come on Milos, open this door!"

"I am," he replied grouchily as he unlocked his door and opened it. He froze when he saw Dimas with a look of mingled fear and anger on his face. A palace guard stood close behind him.

For a second Milos thought they might be there to arrest him. But a moment later Dimas leaned forward and pulled Milos into a hug.

"Thank the stars," Dimas said in a whisper. He released Milos and took a step back. Milos realized that he was standing in his underwear.

"We feared they might have been going after you," Dimas explained. Milos had no idea what this meant. His look of confusion must have shown on his face because Dimas began to smile a little.

"I might have known, you slept through all this madness," Dimas said. As he spoke another guard ran passed them. Milos could hear chattering voices from down the hall.

"Milos, the palace has been attacked!" Dimas said, "And the culprit may still be inside the palace. We've been searching but have yet to find anyone." Dimas looked worried again. He paused then asked, "Milos, did you lock your door?"

At this, the guard pushed past both of them and began to look around the room. Milos was annoyed at this intrusion until he realized that the guard was looking to see if anyone else was in his room. As the guard opened the closet to look inside, he turned back to Dimas.

"Yeah, I, uh, locked it last night," he said to Dimas. Dimas looked over at the guard who indicated that there was no one else in the room.

"Good, good," Dimas said distractedly. Then returning his attention to Milos, "Very good, in fact. That may have saved your life!"

"Milos, we are going to leave a guard posted outside your room until we are sure the palace is safe," Dimas said. Milos had no desire to go anywhere and nodded his head. The guard stepped back out of the room.

"Just wait here, Milos. I'll be back to check on you later," Dimas added quickly before turning and hurrying down the hall.

Milos looked up at the guard framed in the doorway. For a fleeting moment, he thought he was looking at the same guard he had seen pulling his partner across the grounds. No, this man was taller. His shoulders were with wider.

The guard did not say anything, but turned his back to him and began watching the hallway. This was fine as far as Milos was concerned. He did not want to talk, and besides that, he preferred to have his pants on when meeting new people.

He closed the door and began walking back towards his bed. It was still early morning. He didn't know how much time had passed since he collapsed on his bed. It could not have been long.

He looked out the windows and saw warm sunlight falling on the faces of the distant mountains. There was still an odd silence in his room, though Milos could hear all sorts of sounds coming up from the floor below.

He was still exhausted, but found he was thinking more clearly now. The fire no longer seemed to be swirling inside his head. He decided that he must have been in shock when he had gotten back to his room. He had read about such things happening to soldiers in battle.

Part of him desperately wanted to go back to his bed, but he was beginning to realize the severity of the situation. He could not go to sleep and hope everything would blow over. The whole palace was in an uproar thinking they were under attack, fearing some sort of coup or assassination attempt.

He doubted the chaos was limited to the palace. All those people he had seen on the streets before dawn must have seen the massive fire. What would they be thinking? Dimas seemed to think that someone was using magic to attack the palace.

The search for the attacker would turn up nothing of course, because there was no attack. At least not an intentional one. Someone had been hurt. Illegal magic had been performed. And only Milos knew what had really happened.

He tried to imagine what everyone would do when no explanation for the attack could be found. Then he realized with a jolt that the Lady Keren and her entourage were due back at the palace later that day. Had she seen the spell? What would she think it meant? She obviously knew someone had stolen a bottle of the blue liquid from her bag last night.

She might think it was some plot of Lord Andrik's. That he meant to blame her for an attack on the palace. Unless she thought to question Caleb first. Of course she would. Would Caleb keep his secret or would he admit to showing Milos the spell? If he told her what they had done, she would know Milos knew about the secret compartment.

He took a deep, resigned breath. He tried not to think about the consequences of what he was about to do. He knew it was his duty to do it. He walked over to his closet and put on fresh clothes. He retrieved the folded plan of the Karpat and transferred it to the pocket of his new pants.

He closed his closet door and moved behind his bed and ducked down low. He quietly retrieved the bottle of blue liquid from the box beneath his bed. He barely looked at it as he slid it into his pocket. He was becoming furious with himself for having treated it like some kind of toy.

Milos stood up and smoothed out the front of his clothes with his hands. Then he walked over to his door and pulled it open. The guard outside turned around at the sound of the door opening. He looked down at Milos, and with a gruff, urgent tone he asked, "Is everything alright?"

Milos hesitated for a second then replied.

"Yes, everything is fine in here."

"Good," the guard replied, "stay calm until we get this sorted out, Master Baran"

Milos didn't move but instead took a deep breath before finally saying, "I need to speak to my father." He tried to speak with as much authority as he could muster, but he was not sure how well he had managed it. At any rate, the guard did not seem moved by the declaration.

"I'm afraid that will have to wait," he replied flatly.

Milos did not think it would be a good idea to wait for the all clear. Who knew when they would give up the search. The palace was large with many rooms.

He had to think of a different approach. He thought for a moment and then asked,

"Can you tell me, sir, did he survive?"

"Did who survive?" the guard replied suspiciously.

"The man who was burned by the fire, did he survive?" Milos asked with genuine concern in his voice.

"How did you know about that?" the guard

asked. Milos did not respond. Eventually, the guard answered.

"Last I heard he was alive. He was rushed off to the physicians at the barracks."

Milos nodded and waited for the question to come again.

"How did you know about that, Master Baran?" The guard repeated.

"I must speak with my father," Milos said in response to the question. The man narrowed his eyes and looked at Milos appraisingly.

"It's urgent, I must speak with him immediately," Milos said, desperation now edging into his voice. After a long pause, the guard spoke with a tone that suggested he was acting against his better judgment.

"Follow me."

# 18: The Truth

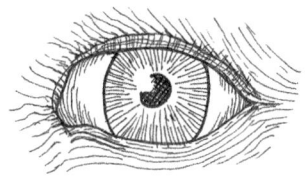

Milos followed the guard down the hallway towards the main stair. They reached the point where the wall to their left gave way to a wrought iron railing. His escort stopped and looked down at the main hall below. It was filled with men guarding every path into and out of the main hall.

They all stood around nervously as there was no sign of trouble so far. This did not surprise Milos of course, but the guard escorting him wanted to make sure all was clear. Once he observed the relaxed alertness of the men below, the guard continued on to the stairs. He moved down them at a steady pace, taking one stair at a time.

Once they reached the bottom, the guard stopped once more to observe the hall carefully. Milos was not exactly eager to reach his destination. Still, he felt irritated with the guards cautiousness.

He kept forgetting that he was the only one who knew the palace was not under attack.

At last, the guard continued, crossing from the stairs to the door into his father's study. Milos could hear many voices deep in debate on the other side. The guard glanced back at him to make sure he was still close to him, and then knocked on the door.

The chatter behind the door continued unabated. Just as the guard raised his hand to knock again, the door opened a few inches. An urgent and impatient voice came through the narrow opening of the door.

"Yes, what is it?"

"Lord Andrik's son wishes to speak to his lordship," the guard replied.

Milos saw a pair of eyes look down at him through the gap. He was one of his father's ministers. Milos could not remember his name.

The man had an irritated look on his face but pulled the door open anyway. He allowed the Milos and the guard to step past him into the room and closed the door. The sound of many overlapping conversations continued without regard for the new arrivals.

Milos had been in his father's study from time to time, usually when his father felt the need to share some important lesson on the arts of governing and statecraft. The room was long and narrow with a large wooden table at the far end. Lord Andrik stood at the head of this table, silhouetted by the rising sun. He was in heated conversation with several advisors.

Many other member of his staff sat in discussion all along the table. Others were seated on the plush chairs at the near side of the room. He stood patiently, but no one paid him any notice. The guard who had escorted him there seem to feel his role had been fulfilled and stood quietly by the door.

Eventually, Milos began the slow process of making his way across the crowded room to where his father stood. He had made it about halfway down the length of the table when the door to the study opened dramatically. Several people stopped talking and turned to look as Dimas entered the room with a heavy silence.

When Lord Andrik looked across the table towards him, he began to speak.

"Sir, we have found evidence of a spell being cast inside the palace." There were several gasps around the room, their worst fears apparently confirmed. "In the cellar," Dimas continued, "they found a strange burn upon the floor and the ceiling above. They called me there, and I confirmed that the marks were not made by natural fire."

"Do you know the nature of this spell?" Andrik implored him.

"There is little to judge by. There was no real damage to the cellar, so we must assume its purpose is more subtle, perhaps even benign."

"I doubt that anyone would force entry into the palace, and through such dangerous means, without ill intent."

Dimas nodded gravely in response. After a moment's thought, he spoke again.

"I fear that the culprit is no longer in the palace. If we cannot locate them, we are unlikely to divine the purpose of the spell. Not until it is too late to counteract it." A long silence followed these words. At last, the room was actually quiet.

Milos cleared his throat loudly. Every set of eyes

in the room turned towards him. His heart was pounding so hard he suspected everyone in the room could hear it.

"Milos, what are you doing here?"

It was his father speaking.

"I...I need to tell you something," Milos said. He took a deep, steadying breath. "I know who cast the spell."

Everyone in the room continued to stare at him. Most of their faces were incredulous, but they all looked eager to hear his story. He cleared his throat again and said,

"As for the spell in the cellar, Caleb cast it. I saw him do it." Milos thought it would be best to begin with Caleb's spell before confessing his own. But, this came with a pang of shame for betraying the trust Caleb had shown him.

Andrik exploded at this.

"Lady Keren's son! Are we betrayed by the very guests we welcomed into our city?"

"No! You don't understand," Milos replied frantically. "He wasn't trying to do anything bad, he just wanted to show me a spell. He was, you know, showing off or something."

"Not doing anything bad?" Lord Andrik barked "What about the man lying in a hospital bed in the barracks? Is that another misunderstanding?" he shot at his son. Milos understood why his words had angered him. His father didn't understand why Milos was defending someone who was clearly their enemy.

He had hoped to soften the blow by redirecting his father's anger at Caleb first, but that had backfired. It was too late now, he had to explain.

"That was a mistake," Milos said, speaking loudly and clearly. He did not want there to be any doubting who was responsible for this mess.

"But it was not Caleb's mistake, it was mine."

The room fell into silence again. Not so much as a bird chirping outside the window.

"Caleb showed me the spell in the cellar. But I was the one who cast the spell in the courtyard. It was me."

The room was still locked in a stunned silence. Milos reached into his pocket and pulled out the small bottle, half full of glowing blue liquid. Then he set it down firmly on the wooden table in front of him with a satisfying clunk. The sound punctuated Milos's confession and, he thought, proved it to be true.

Most people stared with interest and wonder at the bottle. Dimas dashed forward immediately. He knelt down next to Milos, examining the bottle closely without touching it.

"Caleb gave this to you?" Dimas asked urgently.

"Um, not exactly" Milos replied slowly. "Last night, after everyone was asleep. I snuck out of the palace and went down to the Karak. I had seen where Caleb had gotten the stuff from his mother's case."

"Ah, now I see why you were so curious to know where they were staying," said Dimas knowingly. "But it was foolish to go there alone" his tone suddenly severe. "If you knew about this danger, why didn't you tell us?"

"I didn't realize how dangerous it was until this morning," Milos said. He felt fully aware of what a fool he was making of himself.

"It seemed like a simple trick when Caleb showed

it to me. I wanted to try it for myself. And when I got back to the palace and saw the doors guarded, I thought I could use it as a distraction to sneak back inside, but..." Milos trailed off.

Lord Andrik had so far said nothing since his son's confession. Milos had been speaking to Dimas, but now turned to look at his father. He expected to see anger on his father's face. Disappointment. Shame. But his father seemed deep in thought, wearing a look of great concern.

"Milos, you say you got this bottle from Lady Keren's case. Was there more of it?" He asked with a calm but serious tone, motioning towards the bottle on the table.

"Yes," he replied relieved that he was not being yelled at. "I didn't count them, but there were two dozen at least." Andrik exchanged a dark look with Dimas. Then he turned to the guard by the door

"Bring the Lady Keren to the palace, and be sure to bring this case as well."

# 19: Confrontation

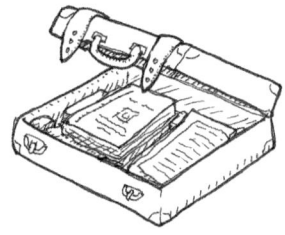

The guard turned and left the room immediately. As the door closed, Dimas carefully lifted the glass bottle up off of the table. He examined it more closely as he stood up again, then hurried over toward Lord Andrik. They immediately began a hushed conversation and paid Milos no more notice.

He had expected raised voices and punishment. He expected everyone to be mad at him. He had not expected to be shunted aside after revealing such scandalous information. He also thought everyone would be relieved that there was no attack.

Some people around the room did seem to relax a bit, but this was tempered by Lord Andrik's demeanor. If anything, he looked even more worried than before. Milos couldn't understand why. His father turned to address the room.

"We must be very delicate in how we handle

this situation," he said seriously. "I think it best if most of you would return to your rooms for the time being." Then Lord Andrik motioned to a handful of his closest advisors, directing them to remain in the study with him. Milos turned to leave and return to his room, a bit bewildered by all of this.

"Milos," Lord Andrik called after him. He turned back and faced his father.

"You better stay as well. Sit in the corner here and do not speak unless I call upon you." He directed Milos to a straight-backed chair set beside the windows. Milos walked to the corner and sat down. He felt a bit better when Dimas moved to stand next to him. It felt like everyone was taking their positions, anticipating Lady Keren's arrival.

After a surprisingly brief wait, the door to the study opened up, and a guard stepped in. He had a leather case in his hand. Milos recognized it at once. The guard sat the case before Lord Andrik. He explained that the Lady Keren would be arriving shortly with some of her entourage. Milos wondered if this would include Caleb as well.

Milos was not eager to see him again. His confession would undoubtedly get Caleb in trouble as well. If not with Lord Andrik, then with his own mother. Milos had so far avoided any mention of the other contraband he had hidden in his room. But Caleb might reveal this secret in retaliation for his own betrayal.

When the party arrived, however, Caleb was not with them. Only three men followed behind the Lady Keren, who was fuming. As soon as she saw Lord Andrik, she began to voice her displeasure.

"What is the meaning of this! Dragging us from our rooms like criminals!" she spat at Lord Andrik.

Lord Andrik did not speak but instead unlatched the case in front of him. He began examining its contents one at a time before setting each item aside on the table. The Lady Keren started to protest in outrage

"You have no right to examine my belongings. How would you answer for this insult!"

Milos sat quietly in the corner as he was instructed, and was using the time to appraise the situation. He was beginning to understand better now. Lady Keren was playing the victim. But she must have suspected that Lord Andrik already knew what was concealed inside the case. Still, she would not give anything away unless her suspicions were confirmed. She was very shrewd.

Milos also began to understand his father's concern now. The Lady Keren had promised a great friendship between Anadel and her own city. Even his father had seemed to believe her intentions were good. But Lord Andrik was also shrewd, and this strange turn of events had put him on his guard.

What if she was only pretending at friendship? If her intentions really were nefarious, what was she planning to do? Especially with all this dangerous blue stuff which she had smuggled into the city?

Dimas was still standing next to him. Milos reached out and tugged his sleeve.

Dimas bend down to put his ear next to him.

"Inside the rim of the lid, there is a concealed button. It opens a hidden compartment," Milos whispered so that only Dimas could hear him. Dimas stood up and approached the table. The case was almost empty now. Andrik was rifling through the pages of a journal, ignoring Lady Keren's objections. Dimas reached across him and felt searchingly behind the lip of the case. In a moment the false panel fell forward into the near empty case.

A bright blue glow washed over Andrik and Dimas. They were looking down at what Milos knew were rows of glowing glass bottles. He could not see them himself, Dimas was now blocking his view. Andrik grabbed the whole case and turned it towards Lady Keren. The scowl on her face looked grotesque in the blue light.

She gave a sharp huff through her flared nostrils and crossed her arms defiantly.

"Well, don't pretend to act surprised Andrik, as if you brought me here on a whim. I know you had one of your men break into my room last night. I returned to find every door and window unlocked. Sloppy work," she jabbed.

"I gave no such order my lady," Lord Andrik replied flatly.

"Indeed not!" Keren replied incredulously, "and what is more, I found some of my property was stolen, and now I think I see why. I'm told there was some fiery apparition over the palace this morning. No doubt you conjured it yourself so that you could accuse your guests of an attack?"

"I do not know who conjured this apparition," Andrik said. Milos's whole body stiffened in his chair. Was his father lying to protect him?

"Indeed," Andrik continued, "we have spent much of the morning searching for the culprit. When they could not be found, we compiled our suspects and found the list to be short."

"And no doubt you also guessed by chance there was something hidden in my case?" Lady Keren replied derisively. "What I keep within my luggage is my own affair. I am not some common peasant. You had no right to search my things, whatever silly laws about magic you wish to uphold in Anadel."

"That may well be true, were it not for an apparent attack on the palace this morning. Whether it was done by your orders or not, you have brought this destruction into my city," Lord Andrik said gesturing towards the case in front of him.

"So we come to it then. You can deny that you violated the sanctity of my room without pretense. But your words confirm my suspicion. This is a plot of yours. You have spied and stolen and are trying to implicate me of some crime. The king will hear of your treachery, Lord Andrik," she spat his name with disdain.

Lady Keren turned to leave the room. At first, a guard made to stop her from going, but Lord Andrik waved him off and allowed Keren to leave the room.

"Make sure our guests do not linger in the city. It is time for them to move on," Lord Andrik said to the guard once Lady Keren was out of the room. The guard gave a nod, and then followed her out the door.

Milos was not sure if being a noble person really did put Lady Keren above the law banning magic. His father had not refuted that assertion. Milos began to feel a bit of sympathy for Lady Keren. If she really had not broken the law, then his father was putting the relationship between Anadel and Breen at risk. Just to shield his son from the consequences of his actions.

This thought made him feel awful. He had half a mind to run out of the room and confess everything he had done to the Lady Keren. But then he thought better of it. His father had already told the lie. If he tried to refute his father now, it could make things worse. He had caused enough trouble. He remained quietly in his seat.

Lord Andrik spun the case around to examine the glowing bottles again. Milos wondered why the Lady Keren had not insisted that her property be returned to her. Instead, she had left her case, the bottles, and all the papers inside it behind.

"Stars above, I've never seen so much. There must be over two quarts here," Dimas said in a whisper.

"Yes," replied Andrik, "we must determine what it's intended purpose was. I fear I already know."

# 20: Broken Things

Lord Andrik and Dimas began to discuss what was to be done with all of the items now strewn across the table. Milos wanted to leave but felt he could not. He felt like he still had not done what he had come here to do, even though he had already confessed everything he had done.

He had caused a huge mess. Not only by injuring the guard and setting off a panic, but now his father had insulted their guests to cover up for him. Yet for some reason, no one seemed that bothered by what he had done. For that matter, they appeared to have forgotten he was there.

Milos stood up and cleared his throat again. Lord Andrik and Dimas stopped talking at once and turned to face him.

"Father," Milos began, trying to keep his voice from faltering, "I'm...sorry."

At first, his father did not seem to understand, but then comprehension began to dawn on his face.

"As you should be," Lord Andrik said.

His father grabbed the chair that was pushed under the table and pulled it out so he could sit level with Milos.

"Sneaking out of the palace. Breaking into the Karak. Stealing. Playing with magic!" He paused a moment. "But that is not the worst thing you have done, Milos."

Milos was shocked by these words. He was sure that performing an illegal spell was the ultimate crime in his father's eyes. When he did not respond, His father continued.

He pulled one of the glass bottles from the case and held it up. "Your biggest mistake was not telling us as soon as you found out about this."

"There is enough silias in this bottle to blow up the whole palace, or do all manner of terrible things," Lord Andrik said.

Milos's eyes were wide with shock. He remembered thinking he might have blown up the palace by accident, and this only confirmed it.

"I didn't know, I'm sorry," he said lowering his gaze. His father let out a long sigh of resignation.

"I understand, Milos. You wouldn't know because I didn't want you anywhere near this sort of thing." Andrik returned the bottle to the case.

"I have forbidden Dimas to teach you about magic, particularly because you seem to have such a great interest in the subject. Perhaps that was a mistake..." Andrik's attention drifted for a moment as he looked back at the case.

"If we had known sooner, perhaps we could have learned more about what Lady Keren is really up to. But at the very least, you did give us enough warning to stop whatever it was for now."

"But, how do you know she was up to something?" Milos asked, "Is it true what she said, that she can carry what she likes because she is a Noble?"

"In a manner of speaking she can. It would normally be frowned upon to search a fellow Noble. But I warrant the spell from this morning gave me justification to do it. As to your first question, I have no doubt she is up to something. Take this for example," Lord Andrik reached out and grabbed a piece of paper from the table and showed it to Milos.

It was a map of the palace. In fact, it looked as though it might have been taken from the same book as the map in Milos's pocket. Milos retrieved it and compared the two.

"There are other suggestive things here," Lord Andrik continued, "but nothing more so than the immense quantity of silias she was carrying. I shudder to think what she might have planned to do with it. Trust me, Milos, we can be sure that Lady Keren is no friend to Anadel if she brought this here."

His father stood up.

"In fact, the first thing to be done is to get this stuff out of the city. Gathering so much magical power in one place is unwise. It upsets the balance of the city. That alone could cause us problems."

Dimas put his hand on Milos's shoulder.

"That much I have taught him," Dimas said. "Let me escort Milos back to his room, then I will arrange proper transport for our unwelcome goods."

Lord Andrik nodded to Dimas and then turned

to Milos.

"Don't think you have avoided punishment for your actions, Milos," Lord Andrik said. "It will take more thought than I can spare at the moment to decide on the appropriate consequence for such outrageous behavior."

"Yes sir," Milos said, bowing his head again. He felt he deserved whatever was coming to him.

"And Milos?" Andrik added "Thank you. I believe we prevented a great disaster today, and you have revealed a great threat to our city."

Milos gave his father a faltering smile, then Dimas led him out of the room.

They walked in silence all the way back to his room. Once they were inside, however, he began to question Dimas.

"Dimas, what will happen if Lady Keren complains to the King like she said?"

Dimas responded with a laugh.

"That was a bluff. She wouldn't dare stand before the king and invite questions about what she was doing here with a case full of silias. This is a matter to be settled between our cities. The king prefers not to get involved if he can help it. His influence over the great cities is not what it once was."

Milos hesitated for a moment and then asked.

"But, what is that silias stuff?"

Dimas wagged his finger at Milos reproachfully.

"Perhaps we will speak more of it if your father changes his view on the matter. Besides, you seem to know quite a lot about it already."

Dimas was giving him a wry smile, but Milos frowned.

"What will happen to the guard? The one who I..."

Milos trailed off unable to finish the question.

"He is alive, and I see no reason that will change now. Likely he will make a full recovery. Though I suspect the magic will leave some mark on him, whether seen or unseen," Dimas replied. Milos did not completely understand what he meant, but he was not eager to pursue the topic any further.

"After all," Dimas continued "it was an incredible display of magic." The wry smile returned to his face. "In fact, the thing which I find most impressive is that you were able to repeat such as spell after only seeing it performed one time."

Dimas's was observing him carefully. Milos was pointedly avoiding his teacher's eyes. Dimas must suspect that he was still hiding something, which was true. He was hiding something just across the room under his bed.

Milos was not sure what he should do. If he revealed his hidden books, Dimas would probably confiscate them. Milos did not want to give up his spell books. He did not think there was any danger in the books by themselves, but he also did not want to lie to Dimas. Not after today.

Just as he was deciding that he may as well come clean about the books, Dimas broke the silence.

"I'm sure we will have a chance to discuss it in more detail later. For now, there is work to be done. The effects of today's events will be far-reaching. Many things are likely to change, and we must be prepared."

Milos looked up at Dimas. He did not find these words comforting and was surprised to see that

Dimas was still smiling down at him.

"I will likely be away from the city for a few days. In the meantime, I expect you can carry on with your studies on your own. If you will excuse me," and with a nod Dimas turned and walked out of the room, closing the door behind him.

Milos was alone again, and he felt his exhaustion return all at once. It was about time for breakfast. He was sure Old Bina would have made sure food was prepared, even in all the uproar. But he was not hungry. All he wanted to do was sleep.

He walked over to the side of his desk. It was still covered with the map he had laid out there. As he looked at it, he wondered what Caleb and Lady Keren were doing now. Maybe they were already traveling up the river, or perhaps in their carriage heading east. Back to Breen.

The case of silias was leaving the city as well. Where would Dimas take it? Would he destroy it? Or would he simply store it somewhere safe? Somewhere far from Anadel.

He looked over to the corner of the map and picked up one of the books. He opened it to a spot where a page had been torn out. He took that page out of his pocket and set it, still folded, inside the book. Then Milos closed the book, set it down.

Reaching across the desk, he closed the curtains to block out the light. Then he walked across the room, crawled into his bed, and fell fast asleep.